Phaneron

The Tragedy of Demolache

Marc Laton

This is a work of fiction. Names, characters, businesses, places, events, and incidents are either the products of the author's imagination or used in a fictitious manner. Any resemblance to actual persons, living or dead, or actual events is purely coincidental.

Cover Illustration by Sean R. Spencer

ISBN: 0692403817
ISBN-13: 978-0692403815

TABLE OF CONTENTS

By the Phaneron I mean the collective total of all that is in any way or in any sense present to the mind, quite regardless of whether it corresponds to any real thing or not.

—C.S. Peirce

 **PROLOGUE**

An hour ago we were throwing back pints of draft Miller and watching young comedians make careers of things they had scribbled on napkins. Now she was getting undressed before my eyes. Maybe it was something I said. She called me charming when I offered to buy her dinner. She called me sweet when I complimented her punctuality. She called it a coincidence when I told her I liked the same music as her. It was all too easy. As she got on top of me and we began rolling around in her bed, I remember trying to think of the most horrid things to say. Things that would make angels cry. Perhaps I could compliment the fact that she kisses well despite her gap teeth, or tell her that real tits are overrated anyway. It was like a shadow took over my mind at times like these. It was a constant game of how can I ruin another night. It was a game that had no winner—a game rooted in an internal war, five years in the making.

"I'm not doing this," a voice declared from the other side of the room, filling me with instant pain and sorrow. He was a tall blonde man—or monster—depending on your position. His eyes pierced souls with their neon blue glow. He was something of a sinister judge, a man lost to the trials he faced and was unable to overcome. Demolache. The wanderer, the warrior, and the wrath himself.

"I can't do this," I said as I clawed at my heart and began to shiver. It was as if his words had come out of my mouth. Like God speaking through me. My mind forever in conflict and this pain never ending. As Demolache smiled and shook his head, I was filled with the emptiness of a gutted carrion. My organs were splayed in front of me like some sort of offering.

Another persona raged in protest. "What the fuck, Demolache? Just give it a chance. I'm trying to show you that there is still hope. What you felt was lust, and you need to get over it instead of dwelling on the past. For Christ's sake, why the fuck am I even still trying to convince you?" This voice came from a dark haired boy, once abandoned in my mind for several years but recently uncovered almost by accident. His eyes were red and not piercing, they burned with something other than rage: ambition. This was Ozymandias. The Shahanshah himself.

"This isn't going to prove anything. It is a waste of time and unnecessary," Demolache replied to Ozymandias's outrage. He felt reassured that he still had the upper hand.

"I'm sorry. I just need a cigarette," I told her as I left the room, struggling to get my clothes on and my head together. Confused like a teased puppy, she let out a scoff as she covered her nudity with wrinkled sheets.

I staggered out of the room and made my way out the front door. Half drunk and half frustrated, I lit a cigarette as I stumbled into the street and screamed, "You two have been a pain in my ass for the last two months, and this is the third time something like this has happened! I never minded when you were just voices in my fucking head, but now you are ruining my life! I can't take it anymore!" I needed sleep. I needed peace of mind.

"I need to end this crazy war before I get committed."

The two were fighting an epic battle in my mind for control, locked in a state of attrition, each trying to convince the other to give up. It was trench warfare, and I was stuck in no man's land. My life had become a mess since this all started, and it was all because of that Flower. She had been, for a time, Demolache's purpose. A vision of heaven amidst all the hell. He had convinced himself of her perfection, and now that she was gone, withered and perverted by his own demons, Demolache had new plans. He had found a new purpose. Destruction in the name of God's divine will. A proverbial flood for the sake of moral purification. How he wanted to accomplish this was the worst part of all.

"You have to understand that what you had was a lie that you convinced yourself of. I don't know how else to prove that to you other than to make you experience it all over again," Ozymandias said. His laugh was something of a desperate gasp. He was beginning to lose hope in all of this. He couldn't however. He refused to lose. Hope was all he had.

"So is this who you think I am? Just some whore's one night stand because you are too afraid to accept me? Give up this pity party and let me do what I need to do," Demolache commanded.

Ozymandias ground his teeth in frustration. "That's not at all what this is about! I just want you to let things go.

Realize that it was all lust. Realize that you, too, are flawed! Please do not go through with this!"

I started to believe that an asylum was what I needed since I was talking to my imagination at two in the morning in the middle of the goddamn street. If anyone were to look into my mind at this point in my life and see what war was raging inside, they would have mercy killed me as they would an old man unable to overcome the pain of his cancer, like my Grandfather. But no, that was his choice, and it wouldn't be mine.

"I wish I could go back to that moment and save myself before you were ever created," Ozymandias retorted, spitting at Demolache's feet. "I don't even understand why you are still here. I don't need you anymore. I never will again."

With the force of a god, Demolache cracked his knuckles against Ozymandias' jaw, knocking him to the ground. "Don't act like you are superior! If you had it your way, I would be nothing more than a heathen who gambled everything away! We would have nothing! You're just a war-monger. A dreamer whose dreams only serve himself. You could never even imagine how I feel!"

I closed my eyes, pulled at my hair, and raised my voice. "Stop it, both of you! We need to go home. We need to end this. We are not going to talk about this anymore. Since she left, all you two have done is argue. Demolache, she's gone. Ozymandias, this isn't the way to get over her."

When I opened my eyes, they were gone. At least I could still control them temporarily.

I started walking the lonely streets of the city, seeking more signs of civilization: a car, a street light, even another person would have been nice. I needed to get home. I needed to stop this battle. Was Demolache my morals and

Ozymandias my ambition? No, they would be able to coexist if that were true. I didn't understand anymore. Who was I? This phaneron? This phage? If neither, then some sort of phantom? I was something existing between worlds divided. A hollow ghost of my former self, cursed to walk in my own version of liminal reality. That, or maybe I had just fucking snapped for the second time in my life, and I was seeing physical manifestations of the militant forces in my soul. They had cost me everything—my education, my future, my sleep, my pride. If I didn't end this war, I would be dead within the month. When had they started controlling my life? As hard as I tried, I couldn't remember. Fuck, why couldn't I remember? Since "The Flower," as Demolache called her, had left, they had been in a constant battle for control of my thoughts, and now I couldn't think straight. I was slowly going insane. Wearing only one sock and my shirt on inside-out, I finally managed to hail a cab home. "12th and Evarts please," I said, clawing my fingers through my hair again. When I got home, however, I didn't find much solitude.

Ozymandias broke the silence as I rested my head on my pillow. "We can't give up hope. It's all we have left. I understand that you are angry, but your ends don't justify the means," he said, rubbing his jaw, which was still in pain.

"Why not? It's not like I need any of them. All these heathens and sinners are corrupting me. The Flower was the only thing worth preserving, and now she's ruined," Demolache remarked as he lit his cigarette.

"No! No more of her! No more goddamn fighting, we need to figure this out diplomatically. If The Flower could break me like this, then the only way to fix this is to undo her from my life. Let's start from the beginning. How did this war begin? Who am I? Who are WE?"

They both looked at me as if they heard me for the first time in two months. Unable to answer, however, they shrugged and stared at the ground quietly. Eventually, a moth entered the room searching for light. Its wings flapped violently as it jack-knifed about the room. As if it were the great Odysseus returning to Ithica or Gilgamesh to Uruk, triumphant but weary, it desperately sought rest. It finally settled upon Ozymandias' shoulder as I watched with teary eyes.

"You should know who I am," Ozymandias finally said, standing up and making for the door. "I think what will really scare you, is who *he* is."

"I really don't care where we start. I just want it all to end," I said, rolling onto my stomach.

Ozymandias stopped at the frame of the door and sighed. "I just wanted you to see that it doesn't matter anymore, Demolache, but fine. Go ahead. Let's hear you dwell in the past because you refuse to let it go. Let's hear how pathetic you really are. I won't be convinced. I will never give up hope."

Something of a sinister smile crept onto Demolache's smoke hidden face. He wanted to remind me. This had been part of his plan all along. "So you want to hear my plea? My argument? My story? All right." He stared at the ceiling and called out, "Calliope, it is time to awaken from your slumber." He raised his hands to the sky. "Allow me to spin this tragic tale to my favor. Allow me to convey my sadness, my pain, and my struggle." He glared back at me and growled through the gaps between his teeth, "*Musa, mihi causas memora*, if you are willing. I'll make you understand, I'll show you how things actually happened." He then sat at my bedside and blew a dark and twisted puff of gray smoke. "Close your eyes and open your mind, it's about to get epic."

His words become hypnotic. My eyes began to gain weight, there was no more resistance. I felt my mind leave reality as I rewound the last six years of my life. I felt myself becoming Demolache, this long-ingrained sense of righteousness which I could no longer suppress. His anger and pain. His deep, soul-piercing blue eyes. His deep self-hatred that burned inside like the first embers of a great forest fire. Everything went black as I heard the crash of waves all around me. I smelled the bitter scent of sorrow in the air.

Part One: The Fall

5.5 Years Ago

SESSION I: THE MAN

PREMONITION ONE

Demolache stood on the rope bridge that lay before him. The high winds and rain seem to have held him back, but he stepped forward anyway. Was this the end of his journey? The answer that he was looking for? As he walked, he could feel the tension within the jagged ropes, yet he remained at a steady pace as he made his way across. The destination was still unknown as a thick fog covered the island on the other side. Further across, the wind and rain gradually began to intensify until this body started to give in to the intense weight. The bridge began to sway violently, but instead of holding on more tightly he bowed his head to protect his eyes from the rain that pelted this body like bullets. As if the island had roared, the wind thrashed out down the length of the bridge and flung him from his feet. His head hit first, slamming into the wooden cross bars as if he were a smooth rock being cast into the ocean and he began to bleed heavily.

Remaining there for a moment, I thought back to those he had encountered along the way. Wood, the greedy fisherman. Rin the lustful beast of the oasis. Khat, the proud doctor. Resh, the slothful noble. The treacherous wanderer Cat. Edward, the gluttonous priest. They were all heathens who had found a purpose for their lives by unjustifiable means. They were monsters. So was I better than them? I thought to myself. Was I without sin?

He slammed his fist onto the wooden boards and lifted himself, only to lash out. "I don't fear you anymore," he bellowed to the mist and began to run across the bridge at full speed. The wind and rain were as intense as ever, but he seemed unaffected. "I am not the puppet of some false ideal, I have nothing to believe in!" Three-fourths of his way down the length of the bridge, Demolache stopped. The rain had stopped. The wind had stopped. The sun had appeared and, with it, a feeble figure emerged from the end of the bridge.

"Demolache," the figure called to him in a soft voice.

"What is this nonsense?"

"Demolache, don't do this," the figure called to him again.

"What is the meaning of this, stranger?" Demolache bellowed in a fit of rage.

"If you truly were ready, then you wouldn't still blame yourself for his death, you wouldn't still hold such contempt for everything imperfect in this world. You must have hope." And with that, the figure disappeared and the rain and wind returned instantly and harder than ever.

Demolache had collapsed under the pressure of his own wrath. Was it me he was angry at? Or was it his God, whom he had abandoned? Either way, the rage consumed him as he let go a terrifying cry. Just then, he was struck by a bolt of rogue lighting and flung from the bridge into the briny deep.

As water filled his lungs, we thought back to the beginning of his journey. Where did I go wrong . . ?

DEMOLACHE AWAKENS

There was blood. Lots of it. He knelt with his hands in the warmth of it. Clutching at his chest, he found the source—a gash across his chest—and yet people just walked on by. They were faceless forms of flesh with a destination. Too busy to be disturbed. The blood also had a destination. It flowed from his wound with the grace of a majestic snake. It was beautiful; beautiful death. There was a sense of freedom within the rupture. A euphoric high numbed his mind and blurred his vision, and for a second he executed an unfamiliar action: a smile.

His eyes widened as the floor became a portal. He fell, appeasing a weak yearning that he had always felt. As he hit the floor, his eyes closed to find himself awake elsewhere, face down in the cold sand.

In those few moments before the fall, I understood everything: the funeral, God and our destiny. "Fuck it all!" I screamed, and then I was flung into the deep blue like a fallen angel. There was nothing but nightmares. And then, in a blinding flash, there was Demolache. And then . . . I guess . . . He washed up on the African shoreline.

I didn't really remember where his journey began, but somewhere between imagining my own death over and over again and this hell which is how I now saw the world, he had appeared. As if he had always existed and he alone had survived the fall; not me, just him, waking up on that beach. It was special to him, like native soil. I guess he remembered how the sand felt, how the water smelled of salt and the sound of the waves crashing around him. Maybe that's where he first felt free. He thought and therefore he was. It wasn't until morning that he actually moved from that spot. He laid there all night trying to remember what had happened. I remembered wondering if it was a dream but he felt too conscious inside of me for that. In fact, Demolache was never more awake than he was at that moment. It was at that moment that, despite the bleak and hopeless hell of his own existence, he decided to find his own meaning for life. Something to drive him forward. He was sick of blaming himself for everything wrong that had happened in my life. He was going to start anew. Find a new light to chase. And with that last thought and a smile, he drifted back to sleep.

Sweet, sweet sleep . . .

THE AVARICE OF MAN

The seven chambers of the silhouette's revolver spun clockwise. The cylinder rotated, it ground and clicked still. The tension of the poorly lit room amplified such sounds and echoed them back with precise detail. The hand raised the antique revolver to his head. It was clear that this Russian gun hadn't been used for a while, but its reputation ensured its capability. The hammer cocked back, and a faceless chuckle was released from an invisible smirk. Somewhere in the room money traded hands. He searched his killer's face for sympathy but found only abysses for eyes. Six to one weren't terrible odds. The trigger pulled, and the dream ended.

"What the fuck!"

He awoke with the pain of a jagged spear stabbing his ribcage and a large, dark skinned man standing over him.

"You were dead," the figured replied, apathetically.

"Clearly not," he replied, examining his body for damage. He had a small cut where the spear had grazed him on his rib cage. He must have been out for days because the jagged hairs on his chin rivaled the edge of the strange man's spear. He struggled to find footing as sand and salt fell from his body.

"I poke you twice, you dead." The figure shrugged as he returned his weapon to a standby position. "I poke you third time, you alive. I don't understand."

Demolache rose to his feet, and as his eyes adjusted, I saw that the man was no taller than our chin and was difficult to distinguish within a mess of animal hides and colorful feathers. He was very far from home, Demolache thought to himself.

"Where am I?"

The man grinned at him and replied calmly, "You in Wood's new fish spot." Before he could respond, the man intensified his expression and asserted, "I am Wood, there are fish, and THIS is my spot." He nearly yelled as he readied his spear, "You try to take Wood's spot again?"

"No, I just thought it looked like a nice place to nap for a while."

Demolache brushed the sand out of his bleach blond hair and pants as he looked around for his shirt, but it was nowhere in sight. His stomach rumbled with hunger.

"Hey Wood, did you catch any fish today?"

They went off to climb a low hill where Wood had built a small house. The house looked like it was strung together with vines and bark most likely gathered from the nearby jungle. They roasted three fish Wood had caught the day prior. By the time they had eaten, the sun was already going down. That's when Wood asked him:

"Who are you? You don't lick tooth like other one and eyes blue, not red?"

Demolache shrugged and replied, "I wish I knew the answer to that. I feel like I just woke up on the beach, no purpose, no history."

"Mmm, you don't remember anything?" Wood murmured.

"When I try to remember, I just feel this rage. It's like I am running from some idea that I used to hold dear. But now I feel like I'm on a mission to find some new meaning for my life, a reason to wake up in the morning."

Wood shook his head. "Godlessness."

"What do you know about God?"

"I know he good to me when I need him most."

"More than I can say I guess . . . What do you mean when you need him most?"

"I show you."

Wood, with a torch in one hand and a raw fish in the other, took Demolache to the cave just outside the hut. This small, damp cave had the worst odor imaginable, something like rotten fish and sulfur. At the end of the cave was a large, flat piece of rock. Wood brushed off a set of bones that looked like they had been picked clean by rodents and laid down a raw fish.

"Is this your god?"

Wood looked intensely at the rock and said, "One day, I fishing at my father's spot. I catch many, many fish, and when my father ask how many fish? I say none. I sneak off with fish to sell next day but was terrible sandstorm. I walk hopelessly for hours until I get desperate, and then find this rock. I lay all fish on it and ask for God's forgiveness. I pass out and in morning, woke up in father's hut. God gave chance to repent, now I do every day. He save Wood."

"So you brought the stone all the way up here?"

"Wood had house near rock some years later. Right next to good fishing spot. But when I tell people about rock, they bring fish. I take fish and sell back to them. They find out and hurt Wood. I take rock to mountain. It is Wood's rock now, all Wood needs."

"So . . . you live here alone . . . With this rock. You may actually be more insane than I am." Demolache laughed.

"Wood is happy, more than you can say. Life like walk blind in desert, faith is gift of direction."

"Yeah, I'm sure I'd be happy too if I were worshiping some object in a cave," Demolache whispered grumpily under his breath.

Wood didn't reply other than to squint and frown. He then retired to his hut and Demolache camped out at the mouth of the cave. He didn't sleep much that night. He couldn't stop thinking about what Wood said. If life is a blind walk in the desert, there is no way to ever know if you are walking in the right direction. That's when I began to remember it all. That was Demolache's origin. That is where he came from. Sitting alone all night trying to understand my lost faith, seeking purpose after I was abandoned by my grandfather and betrayed by God. There was a time in which I knew the direction I was headed. I had received that present from birth. I had walked that path for so long that I was sure that no matter what I did, it was part of God's plan for me. That's why I was so sure that it was my fault when my grandfather died. It was in God's plan for me that he would die. It all seemed so ridiculous now but I blamed myself and the only out from the pain was to spite God by taking my own life. As if to say, "fuck your plan"; as if to declare that I was in control of my own path. Demolache needed to find something else to fill the void that God left. I had no more morals or direction. He was essentially my replacement for God; he was my directionless morals. Instead of suicide, I found wrath in everything that was wrong in the world.

A VISION OF SIN

He was running through a forest in the middle of the night. Was I chasing something or was I running from something? He looked back to see the outline of a great beast. Running. I was definitely running from that. He glanced back for a second look. Its eyes were burning and red, and it was snarling viciously. The trees were thinning, and he saw a clearing, but he had a strange feeling. Suddenly he saw the edge of the cliff and stopped only for a second as the beast hit him full throttle and both were flung into the abyss.

"Fuck!" Demolache screamed as we were forced awake by a sheet of water.

"You scream when sleeping," Wood said, standing over him with an empty wooden bucket. "But all good, nightmare over." He smirked.

"Yeah because I'm awake now and really fucking annoyed." Wiping the water from his face, he saw that it was still dark out.

"It's time. Go east. Through the dessert. If you leave now, you will make across river before the sands cool."

"What? What is across the river?"

"Take this, you need it, and never stop walking." Wood gave Demolache a wooden shield covered in metal decorations. The decorations seemed to depict some sort of story. "You ever notice the mist? Covers this land. Never quite see beyond it. " And with that, Wood descended the hill with his fishing gear.

"Wait! What is out east? What do you mean about the mist?" Still half asleep, Demolache clumsily chased after him, but Wood was gone. He had disappeared into the fog. Demolache gathered his stuff and began heading east into the vast desert.

As the sun rose, the sands of the desert grew hot as coals. Demolache's feet began to grow dry and red. They burned with the heat of hell itself. He removed the shield from his back for shade and I was instantly struck by an immense fear. What was he feeling? Lifting the shield I saw the words inscribed, "He, out of greed, used salvation for utility." A vision of Wood entered my mind. He was enfeebled and covered in bloody welts with his eyes gouged out and gold dribbling and foaming out of his mouth. The horror left me unable to remember what Wood had looked like previously. Turning over the shield, I saw three depictions: the first was a man holding a rock up in the air in the desert; in the second, people were leaving food and gold at the altar of the rock where a man lay in wait to squander the treasure; and in the third, the man was being stoned to death.

INTERMISSION

"What the fuck?"

For a moment I pulled out of my dreamlike state to think. What memory was Demolache drawing from? Was he trying to show me something I had never seen?

"Demolache, what was that?" I began talking to myself again. It was now four in the morning.

Deep blue eyes in the darkness whispered to me. "You wanted to see your life through my eyes. That was the first moment I saw sin, the greed of man, and that is what it looked like to me."

I shuddered but did not reply. I was too exhausted. It was like a short dream that kicks you awake but just for a moment. Instead of arguing, I drifted slowly to sleep. Sweet, sweet sleep . . . Until tomorrow Demolache. You have my attention for now . . . I just don't understand yet . . .

SESSION II: THE MISSION

All day I thought about what Demolache had shown me. I knew that he existed inside me as a force or a voice, but seeing my life through his fantastical perspective has led me to believe that he always was a distinct personality with a different view of the world. His selective memory, however, had me questioning why these events. What was so special about Wood that it would be his first memory? How much of the six years did Demolache remember? What events triggered his consciousness? And why had he show me that monster?

"Are you ready to continue?" he said, as I got into my bed.

"If this will clarify things, and bring me some sort of calm or peace, then I will listen as long as I have to," I told him.

"You can have peace when we are dead."

THE OASIS

He had wandered too much and could not determine which way was east anymore. He decided to go against what he thought to be the setting sun until he came to a deep valley in the sand.

In the valley was an oasis full of trees and a large pool of water. Wood's warning echoed in our head—"Never stop"—but it was too tempting. He had been walking nonstop for twelve hours now, and we were thirsty. He quickly ran down the side of the valley to get to the water, tripping three times on the way down. When he arrived, he drank from the pool. He drank so much water that he choked and coughed, but he did not stop drinking until he noticed someone behind him.

The soft voice rang in his ear and warmed my body. "Demolache?"

He turned around to see the most beautiful of beautiful women. She was just under his chin with skin that radiated warmth. Her green eyes were like almond shaped pearls that pierced his own with a sweet sense of safety. Her dark hair blew in the wind like careless twirls of lace, and her body was an hourglass of curves that begged to be held. To top it off, she wore nothing but a short pink band of cloth across her breasts, just tight enough to make them peek out a little and an equally tight band of cloth around her waist that stopped mid-thigh. She was godly in all, and the sight of her made Demolache weak in the knees and mind.

"Demolache?" she beckoned again, and his heart nearly stopped beating.

"Hey," he managed to say.

"Demolache, you look tired from your tedious trek through the dangerous desert. Won't you lay with me here? I can ease your soreness."

"I . . . am tired," Demolache said with a dumb smile.

I began to question Demolache. From my memory, Rin did not look that good, but to him, she was Venus herself, I guess. Though I had somehow figured he would have a weakness for women. That much made sense.

The woman took us by the hand and brought him to the water's edge where she entered the pool and began to rub our feet. She rubbed our ankles and our shins. She then beckoned us to enter the pool with her, and he did so . . .

THE MONSTER INSIDE THE MAN

Unbeknownst to Demolache, he spent nine days laying with the harlot before he began to regain his wits. It was on the night of the ninth day, while they were laying together only covered by night's glow, that he finally said, "My apologies woman, but I'm embarrassed that I don't recall ever giving you my name or you giving me yours."

"Demolache, you silly man, everyone knows who you are. You're the great hero returning from your adventure. My name is Rin, the guardian of this oasis."

Her answer seemed a bit generic, seeing as how Demolache was in fact not a great hero but a wanderer and he was on a mission, not an adventure. But those were just technicalities, I guess. In hindsight, I realized, she was talking about Ozymandias. Regardless, Demolache was more than satisfied; he was flattered by her answer. It made him smile and pull her closer to him.

Seven days after that night, or sixteen days after meeting the harlot, she slipped up by drawing attention to the shield and reminding Demolache who he was and what he needed to do. The two were gathering the fruit that seemed to grow on the trees every day—yes, the oasis had apparently turned into the Garden of Eden in the course of sixteen days—when she asked Demolache where he had gotten the shield from.

"A good friend gave me that shield."

"Oh?' She lifted the shield and was noticeably startled upon touching it. "It's ugly, and I don't like it," she said, as she threw it into the water. He failed to catch it, and it sunk to the bottom.

"Why the hell would you do that?" he said, growing angry.

"Oh my gosh, I'm so, so sorry. I didn't think it would go that far, please don't hate me!" She dropped to the floor and began to cry.

"It's okay," Demolache responded, picking her up off the floor and holding her to his body. Later that night, however, Demolache went into the water to retrieve the shield. He looked at his reflection with satisfaction. His beard had now become something of a bramble. The hairs entangled themselves in every direction like a grand thicket long abandoned and under-maintained. Still shirtless, he admired the scars that lay all over his body like an indecipherable treasure map. There were no recognizable landmarks and no "X marks the spot"; just endless roads to be traveled forever. He reached for the shield, but upon bringing it to the surface, I was struck by that sense of fear again. Holding the shield, his reflection was different. It was that of a terrible monster He was engulfed in terrible pain. He was a demon, enfeebled and horned. His skin was a mess of flaking black ash, and his eyes were full of a deep blue fire that smoked as they flickered about like a campfire attempting to stay lit despite the rain. He punched the reflection in anger and tried to hold back his mounting tears.

INTERMISSION

"What the fuck was that!" I screamed as I was once again flung awake by Demolache's sick and twisted version of reality.

"That is who we were! Accept it! You created me in a state of self-hatred and rage, and that is how I saw us," Demolache bellowed from the foot of my bed.

Why did that image make me so angry? Was I always this angry? Was I always such a monster? No, Demolache was, I thought to myself, teeth grinding and fists clenched. He was always a monster from day one. But I needed him to be. I couldn't have done this on my own. I would never have made it. I sighed sadly and lit a cigarette and returned to Demolache's world.

THE LUST OF MAN

He returned to the harlot who was awakened by the commotion.

"What's wrong?" she said in her sweet voice, so concerned, so full of temptation.

"Nothing, let's just go to sleep."

"I don't believe you. You can tell me anything Demolache. I'm here for anything you need or want." She seduced like a serpent.

However, a now shaken Demolache wouldn't fall for this ruse any longer. "Really, I am fine . . . but I'm leaving in the morning."

"Why? Are you not happy? Do I not please you? Do not leave my side, brave hero. I'll simply die without you!"

"Silence," he commanded. "This is not my place. It has nothing to do with you. I must keep going. I must never stop."

"I don't understand," she replied softly.

He remained awake for another hour, reflecting on the image he saw; the monster he truly was. It didn't make sense at the time, but with regard to everything that would happen, it was the truest picture of Demolache I could imagine. The flesh, the face—They were mine, not his . . .

Demolache didn't exactly leave first thing in the morning as he had planned. Instead, he found himself tied to a tree . . . Completely naked. He had misjudged the girl. "What the fuck?"

"There are two ways men leave Rin's oasis," Rin said, wielding a silver blade and spinning it about her finger. Demolache noticed that she was fully clothed in some sort of pink priestess gown and had two heavy bags tied to her waist. Her smooth, silky voice was gone.

"Either your heart will always be mine," she said, as she pointed the blade at his heart. She then dragged the blade gently down his skin until she reached his pelvis. "Or you can never lay with another woman again. Only one has ever left me unscarred."

It was pretty obvious what she meant by that and Demolache preferred the third option. "Are you fucking crazy? What is wrong with you woman! Let me go!" he screamed, shaking his legs free.

"Nothing is wrong with me. It's your kind that are crazy. You treat this oasis as something you can just use and leave. As if we have never yearned for something greater. Well, as long as I guard these waters, a part of you will always be stuck here, with us. If you can't decide, then I'll take my pick." She grabbed onto our manhood tightly, and just before she could slash Demolache freed his leg, and I quickly kicked her in the face and began to shimmy up the tree.

"Shit!" she screamed and started sobbing in her soft, innocent voice. Luckily Demolache was too freaked out by what she had almost done to fall for this. We untied ourselves atop the tree and jumped down to his shield. He picked it up, and suddenly Rin's true form came into my sight. She was a ten-foot-tall giant with six faces that rotated on her spinning neck. The sacks on her side were bloody and full of still beating hearts on one side and sex organs on the other. This sight didn't startle me, however; I felt like I had always knew what she looked like on the inside.

"Don't you love me?" the six heads all said at once as she lifted her blade.

"No one could ever love you, demon!" Demolache screamed as he charged her with his shield. She swung her drawn sword at him. It hit his shield with full force and flung him to the ground. She brought her arm back and then swung her sword into the ground, but Demolache rolled out of the way. Regaining his footing, he hurled his shield at the beast's heads, and it hit with a massive thud as she fell to the floor, releasing her weapon. Without the shield, I saw the harlot as she had been. But when Demolache picked up her sword, she once again became the ghastly beast, and so he thrust the sword through her heart. She let out the cry of a dying animal, like a moose that had been mortally injured but who, out of hope or pain, cries one last time to its brothers and sisters and after a few minutes becomes motionless. A life without lament is a life wasted. On one side of the sword was inscribed, "She, in pursuit of luxury, was so shameless." And on the other side I caught sight of pictures depicting the story of a widowed girl pleasuring men in order to bend them to her will, unable to fill the void her first love had created. All of this because of a grieving heart. How pathetic, Demolache thought to himself.

After dressing himself, minus his shirt, he gathered food and water along with his shield and a new sword. Once again, Demolache began to head east through the seemingly never-ending desert. After six hours, the sun was high in the sky, and the heat was unbearable. We found our way, however, to a great river that stretched as far as the eye could see. The waves crashed violently around one particular part of the river, where it looked like it had been parted somehow. Demolache made his way down the sandy dunes to reach this area, where he found a large stick that had been set into the sand. A moth had chosen to rest upon it. Demolache analyzed the stick with curiosity.

"Whoever you are, I do not need your help," he whispered to himself. He removed the stick from the ground and tossed it to the side. Immediately, the waves began to fill the partition in the river, prompting him to panic. Demolache sprinted full force through the void as water slowly began to rise and restore the river to its former singularity. The water rose past his feet, and then to his knees, and he could run no more. He began to struggle as the water continued to rise until he could no longer touch the bottom. He was but halfway across when he began to drown. Everything went black shortly after but he could have sworn he saw someone jump in after him. Someone who was watching to see what he would do . . .

THE PRIDE OF MAN

Demolache awoke to find himself in a strange bed. The sheets were of the finest silk, and the walls were made of sandstone blocks. Upon rising out of bed, he was struck with a grave pain in his head. He rubbed his temples, but it wasn't long before he realized that he was being watched by a figure sitting in a chair by the door. He quickly made his way to the window on the other side of the room to find that he was in some sort of settlement and it was night time. The moon shone brightly upon the modest homes of this Arabian village.

"You don't sleep much, my friend, do you?" the voice finally broke the silence.

"No, I don't. How did you know?" we replied, remaining fixed on the view of the sky. The moon was full that night, larger than he had ever seen.

"I'm a doctor by trade. I've never seen someone sleep for three days straight. It's as if you can only truly sleep when you are unconscious, my friend. Your body was exhausted," Khat chuckled.

"If you knew where I spent the last couple weeks, you would sleep with one eye open too," Demolache chuckled back. "My name is Demolache, by the way."

"I know who you are. Demolache, the blue-eyed wanderer, right?" he asked rhetorically, standing from his chair. "They call me Khat. It's nice to finally meet you conscious."

I was just as confused as Demolache at this point. "How do you know me?" How did anyone know him? Demolache turned from the window to face Khat, a short haired, darker skinned man. He wore glasses over his solid gold eyes. Startled at this, Demolache searched the room for his sword and shield. "Where are my things?"

The man chuckled. "I do not have your stuff and I did not save you from those waters, but the man who did spoke very highly of you. He said, 'help this fool, and I'll make it worth your while.' He gave me more money than I can spend in a year, my friend."

"Who was he? Did he say how he knew me? What did he look like?"

"Calm yourself, my friend, for these things I cannot tell you. I understand he is a man of mystery in these parts and so I have been sworn to secrecy." He lit a long pipe and began to puff deeply. "What brings you to this proud land, Demolache?"

"I honestly don't know. I awoke on a beach somewhere and was told to just head east and never stop. I need to find purpose in my life. That is my mission."

The man chuckled so hard that he choked on his pipe. "Look no further, my friend, for I am a doctor and have just the cure for godlessness!" The man leapt out of the room. "This way, my friend!"

Demolache followed Khat into the next room. He found him kneeling in front of a golden statue of a calf. "Kneel, my friend, this is the one true god," he proclaimed, with his eyes fixed upon the golden calf.

Demolache observed him kneeling and let out a sigh. "Khat, I have met many men who have said the same, and I once worshiped my own God. I don't think another god is what I am looking for."

Khat, shooting up from his position on the floor, stared him down intensely. "All other gods are false gods, my friend. You have abandoned your god because he was a false god. This is the true god. Worship him, and you will forever be fulfilled by doing his work."

Demolache, put off by Khat's sudden intensity, began to back out of the room. "Khat, to all men, their god is the true god. I'm looking for something deeper. I'm looking to become my own god."

"You dare insult me like this?" Khat began to walk towards Demolache. His eyes were full of prideful rage. "Heathen, there is no other god! And man cannot simply become a god, that is heretical nonsense," Khat said, removing a small dagger from behind his back.

"Relax! Put the knife away! All I said was that I don't need to fall for another religion." His back was against the wall, his muscles tensing at the mounting pressure. Like a threatened snake, Demolache prepared himself for the worst.

"Fall? What do you know of my god?" Khat screamed, charging at Demolache's right rib cage with the small silver dagger. Demolache shifted left, causing the dagger to graze his side instead of piercing his organs.

"Fuck!" We screamed in unison, grabbing the wound and feeling the blood rush. He shoved Khat to the floor. His head hit the wall with a crack, causing the knife to fly from his hand and slide to the other side of the room.

I felt the adrenaline in Demolache's blood. Synchronized, I felt everything he felt at that moment. An unquenchable rage put me in a trance as I felt my eyes glow hot blue. We both stared at the knife and then at Khat, rolling in agony and holding his head. Somewhere inside that man lay a weakness so great, an insecurity so large, that he was compelled to eliminate any threats. The proud fool. But I, too, was proud. Demolache lifted the knife and returned to Khat, grabbing him and throwing him against the wall. The knife in his hand was hungry for blood, and so we drew it back. I was weak, too. I needed this. Khat winced in agony as he saw the knife aiming for his head. His eyes showed his sin. Solid gold, blinded by pride. He was just that, however, a shell; hollow on the inside yet solid on the outside was the beast's true form. A cocoon of self-perpetuating lies. This feeble man latched like a leach onto something greater than himself because he couldn't accept what a worthless creature he really was. "Blinded by pride, he slaughters," the blade read.

I thrust the knife with all my weight, all my anger, with every ounce of rage within my body. I felt the crush of the small blade make contact and pierce the soft stone wall six inches from Khat's head.

"Your god is a lie," I said, one inch away from his face. Still in a trance, I pulled the knife from the wall and dropped it to the floor. Khat began to shudder in fear of the monster that I was and fell to the ground. The back of the blade showed a soldier who fought hard to prove that he had the mandate of heaven but fell easily to the wrath of his enemies. God was not willing in his case. We left the house and headed out into the night.

INTERMISSION

I felt sick and found myself in the bathroom washing my face.

"You liked it, didn't you? The feeling of rage and contempt I felt for them?" Demolache said, standing at the door of the bathroom.

"No, that was fucked up," I responded, staring at my reflection in the mirror. My eyes were dark and baggy. My skin was washed out and pale. I needed to sleep. I couldn't stand this twisted tale any longer. "That's not how it happened, Demolache. I never hurt anyone. I never tried. He was a good friend. Why pervert my memory? Why make things so fucked?"

"What I see is but a metaphor, you are the one who decided to sink your teeth into other people's beliefs. You are the one who made it your personal quest to kill religion or ideology that you found to be stupid or unsubstantiated," Demolache whispered between his teeth.

I caught sight of the blue glow in his eyes. The outline of his body, a reflection of my own. "No," I responded, only half believing my response. "That was you acting through me. I never wanted to hurt anyone. I never meant anything by it." I began tearing up. The pain of the truth was immense. I was not as strong as I thought I was. I couldn't bear much more of this agony.

"You will soon. Shall we return to your enlightenment?"

It was five in the morning. I'd given up on sleep for the night. "Let's just get this over with," I said, wiping my face as I once again closed my eyes and entered Demolache's inferno.

THE SLOTH OF MAN

Demolache's next memory began with him waking up in a palace after wandering the desert for forty days, bleeding and without food or water.

"Where am I?" Demolache said, finding himself on the floor. I looked around the room. The ceiling seemingly reached the heavens, and the walls were regal, white and gold. Paintings of beautiful women danced across the facade.

"Rise, wanderer, and thank your saviors. For we have taken you in as one of our own," a voice echoed across the room.

Rising to his feet, Demolache looked for the source of the sound. His eyes fixed on an ivory throne across the room. A man sat there, garbed in blue silk. He was thin with tan skin and jet black hair. All around him were others in blue silk, standing with golden spears, their faces covered with the fabric.

"Thank you? But where am I?" Demolache repeated.

"You are in my palace, Demolache," the figure on the throne replied. "I am the noble, Resh. We have heard of you and your quest, and we respect you for it."

"Oh? And why is that?" Demolache replied, examining his body. He had a new scar to add to his collection. A gash from the blade of pride.

Resh chortled, "Because we, too, are intellectuals who have long since abandoned our gods in search of something even greater." The room erupted in laughter. "Come now, let's discuss what you have found so far."

Resh, leaving his throne, guided Demolache to the atrium of the palace. They walked in silence for a few moments before Demolache noticed the large claws that extended from Resh's fingers.

"I don't know what you have heard, but I am just a wanderer who has yet to find anything substantial. I can't contribute anything to your group, and I cannot rest until I find something to live for. I must keep moving."

"I see I see. I believe you will find something. Eventually, we all do, and whether it's god or some other meaning, every man must one day find a purpose or remain dead inside forever. The indecisive man will always be a fox," Resh asserted, casually.

"Fox?"

Resh stared at the ground as if pondering whether or not to elaborate. "There is a story I used to hear as a kid; Aesop's "The Fox and the Cat." The Fox thought himself so clever that he bragged to the cat about how many tricks he had up his sleeve while the cat admitted he only had one. When the hounds came, the cat climbed up a tree. The Fox remained, considering his options right up until the hounds tore him apart and the huntsman took him."

Demolache swallowed hard. His Adam's apple sprung against his pale skin. "So . . . What did you find, Resh? What have any of you found?" he returned. "Have you found a purpose for living? Have you become gods of your own existence?" Demolache asked curiously.

"Yes, I have. I live for love. It is the greatest aspect of human nature and the most incredible emotion in our arsenal. I live to feel that feeling, for nothing is greater in this world," Resh said with complete confidence. "Gods? No, we are simply engineers of our own world. Not responsible for creation but for integration, more or less."

"How can things be so simple for you? For any of you?" Demolache said, confused by his answer.

"Because life is far too short to spend too much time always struggling to understand one's own demons," Resh retorted, staring at the sky. "Find something positive and just run with it Demolache, that's what we are all about. Others will struggle, fight, and work their whole lives, but not us. We have settled in order to be at peace within ourselves."

You were right Resh, why couldn't Demolache have understood that? This pity parade, this Sisyphean journey, this pain, this sadness, and this anger; if only he could have let it go. If only Demolache could have seen it that way. He couldn't, however; he could never let go. After realizing this, he replied, "But there has to be more to life than just trying to be happy. What about legacy? What about meaning? Are you saying you have no interest in creating something? Leaving something behind? Becoming someone worth talking about?"

"I did have those feelings once, I just learned to not put too much emphasis on them. You need to choose what defines your life before your life defines itself. Understand? If you are constantly stressing yourself about all of those things, then you will never be satisfied because that will become who you are. Just pick something. Don't shoot for the stars unless you want to become an astronaut. Pick something you can accomplish and go for it." Resh let out an enormous sigh. "Return to the quarters we have provided for you Demolache. Please just think about what I have said. Try to find something that makes you happy. When you find it, return to me, and we will discuss this further. I fear if you don't end this journey soon, the damage will become irreversible."

"If you actually understood me, my pain and my sorrow, you wouldn't insult me by asking me to give up my journey!" Demolache sneered.

"Tell me, great wanderer, what pain is so great that you are unable to see reality anymore? I have met both the man and the monster and am unable to see what strife has warranted the man to convince himself of such fragility that he must hide behind such a beast."

"What are you talking about? Man and Monster?'

"Yes, Demolache, every man is made of parts. You are, but one of these parts, and alone are not a man but a monster. I have predicted your course too, Demolache; your tragedy, your fight, and redemption. Until the phantom comes, you will not be whole. You will be just another face, another monster," Resh asserted before turning his back on him and making for his throne room.

"What the fuck is that supposed to mean? Don't leave me with that! What phantom?"

Resh didn't respond. How could he? He had no way to explain these things to Demolache. Instead, Resh's nobles grabbed Demolache by the arms and guided him to a small room up the stairs of the palace and through a long corridor.

The room was tiny and held only a bed, a toilet, and a sink. He gazed out a small window to look upon the atrium. "It really is about the simple things with you guys, isn't it?" Demolache joked as the figures left.

After the small meal they provided for him, he asked for a razor and a mirror with which to shave. His beard had grown long and unkempt, and it was time to look more civil. To look like . . . A man rather than a beast. He spent an hour removing the months from his chin. How easy it was to make a child out of a monster with only a blade. The small, ornate mirror was decorated with sapphire stones and had the words, *"Veritas libertas est"* engraved on the top. No, Demolache thought to himself. *Veritas tartarus est . . .*

Demolache remained awake all night thinking about what Resh had said. He couldn't ever accept such a simple answer. He needed to create something or destroy something. He wanted to become his own god, and he needed a more complex purpose than mediocrity. There was no way he could settle for something so simple. And what was all that nonsense about parts? He thought, therefore he was. Was that not enough? Was he not a man because he had nothing to believe in?

As Demolache lay awake, he thought about Resh and his crew as well. Such spiritual sloths they were for treating life with rubber gloves. Maybe it was spite, but shame on them for not digging deeper. Shame on them for wasting space on this earth. Sloths, the lot of them. Demolache's disdain began to flare up. He slammed his fist into the pillow. He hated them. The more he thought, the more his rage built until he couldn't take it anymore. He sprang from the bed and looked out the window. Darkness. Lonely darkness was all I saw.

In a rage, he made for the door and followed his way back to the atrium. There was a figure waiting in the darkness, however. It was as if he was expecting us. It was as if he knew everything that had just gone through Demolache's mind.

The figure just nodded and walk away.

Resh must have known that Demolache wouldn't be content with this answer. He must have been waiting for him to leave all night. Did he ever expect him to accept it? Would he have stayed up all night just to find that Demolache had changed? Probably not. Resh had rescued him only to speak his opinion and then wait for Demolache to leave. He predicted this. The nod must have meant that we chose the right answer in his mind. That nod almost calmed Demolache's rage for a moment, but he was too focused on the sin of Resh and his followers. What sloths. What laziness. What complacency. What nothings, he thought. I'm sure they will go on to do great things, but it will all mean nothing if they don't have a reason behind their actions. Love. What is this but a synonym for insanity? Resh, I respect you for understanding my decision, he thought to himself, but I resent you for yours.

Demolache had wandered out of the gates of the palace in his revelry. He never looked back to see the sign on the gates that read, "With great knowledge came great acedia."

East, his heart said. I must keep going east.

INTERMISSION

I sat up to see that the sun had already risen and begun shining through my shade. I lit my cigarette and thought for a while. I was starting to understand where Demolache came from. His consciousness seemed to have been brought on by significant meetings in my past involving the philosophy of life. Was it sheer curiosity? No. He was trying to find something to believe in. A reason to live again. With each such encounter, however, he seemed to grow more and more frustrated with his own lack of purpose. He rejected everyone he met along the way because he saw some sort of sin in their beliefs. Wood was too greedy, Rin was too lustful, Khat was too prideful, and Resh was too slothful. These were good people, however, despite any opinion I had on their beliefs. I guessed that any resentment or frustration I had felt during my conversations with them had just been absorbed and bottled by Demolache. He was building a great hatred for everything sinful or wrong. He must have been leading me to this conclusion. The idea that everyone else was imperfect and ugly and I was too. That was the great cynicism that had lain dormant inside me for so long and which I had never realized. I put my cigarette out and resumed the session to find that he had traveled very far in the five weeks after leaving Resh's palace.

A NEW FRIENDSHIP

Demolache woke from his evening nap encamped in the roots of an old tree, possibly one of the oldest in the forest. He had gotten used to the lifestyle of a nomad, and he had begun gathering whatever resources he could find along the way. A pouch full of berries and fruits, an animal bladder full of fresh water, and a large sharpened stick presumably used for self-defense. He must have been traveling for a long time, as he had almost made it as far east as he could go.

I watched as he rationed his berries for his breakfast, drank lightly from the bladder and then readied himself to continue on with his journey. However, Demolache did not move from that spot for a while. Instead, he stood motionless as if to gain some kind of bearing. He readied his spear and took a step back, staring down his surroundings. For a few minutes I couldn't understand what he saw that had made him so alert, but as I synchronized further into his perspective, I felt what he felt. It was the cold shoulder feeling one gets when they feel as if they are being watched.

He finally called out to the forest, "Show yourself demon! I have nothing but the sharpened end of my stick for a beast such as your –"

"Hello!" a voice pierced from behind his right shoulder, causing him to whirl around and trip on the edge of the very root against which he had slept the night before.

"Identify yourself!" Demolache cried as he fell to the ground into a defensive position with his spear still aimed at the girl. She was very short, with long dark hair and almond eyes. She was wearing an elegant pink dress as if she had just left a party.

"I'm Cat, who are you?" The girl spoke with such enthusiasm that it nearly caused Demolache to drop his guard, but as he picked himself up off of the ground, he remained suspicious.

"You have not heard of me?" Demolache was used to all strangers knowing of him for some odd reason. The fact that this girl was oblivious reassured him somehow. "I am Demolache, the great wanderer! I am headed east."

"If that's the case, you only have another mile or so left to go. The coastline begins at my old village, about a fifteen-minute walk east," the girl replied, now examining Demolache from head to toe.

"What are you saying? Have I finally reached the end of my journey? I haven't found my answer yet." Demolache sat on the ground in a panic to ponder while the girl danced about him in a most childish fashion. Eventually, she tripped and began to cry, but Demolache was too deep in thought to care. "What if I reach the coast and still don't find anything? Where will I go then? Should I attempt to sail? Should I go north? Wood did not give me any further directions."

"You should go north! That's where I am headed," the girl said, replying to Demolache, who had unknowingly spoken aloud.

"But you said your village was to the east . . . what is to the north?"

"My village is to the east, but I'm running away from home to become a nomad," the girl said with a forced smile. "To the north is the mountains. They say that from there you can see the whole world from a clearer view, and there is nothing but the cold to bother you."

"Why are you running away?" Demolache asked, but he did not care for the answer. She talked while he thought about the reply to the second question. A place where he could see the world more clearly. That may be what he needed. A place where people and emotions didn't cloud judgment. A place where he could go to just think. With that, as the girl rambled on, Demolache sprang up and headed northward.

"Wait! Where are you going? Don't leave without me! Did you even listen to what I said?"

"Yeah sure, you ran away from home. I think you should go back home because the world is too far a scary place to be a wanderer," Demolache said, shrugging the girl off.

The girl pouted and crossed her arms. Demolache didn't realize that she had dismissed his suggestion and begun following him from a distance . . .

About a month later, thirty-three days to be exact, Demolache had reached the edge of the trees which opened to a vast steppe. It was then that after waking that morning he noticed something strange. When he reached for his rationed fruits and berries, he found the sack empty. When he went for a drink, he found the bladder gone. He had been gathering supplies regularly during his journey. He had been so careful not to deplete his supply; how could this of happened? Demolache returned to the jungle to collect his supplies again. He would need to collect enough rations to last him across the steppe. A new bladder for water would be nice too, and that meant he would have to hunt. The thought of meat made his mouth water.

Walking through the jungle, I noticed that Demolache passed up most of the berries in this part of the jungle. They were all devil's deception. Poisonous. Demolache had learned through raging diarrhea, fainting spells, and temporary paralysis which ones to eat and which ones not to eat by now. Cat, however, had not, and Demolache soon discovered her half-living body not far from his own camp. She had become too sick from choosing the wrong berries and, in an act of desperation, had stolen his rations and water in the night. Instead of rage, Demolache was overcome with sympathy for the first time in his existence. He gathered what supplies she still had on her and threw her over his shoulder. He then made his way back to his camp, where he gathered the rest of his own supplies and entered the steppe.

Demolache cut down on his food and water rations along the way in order to eventually feed his half-conscious guest for two days before she finally began to regain consciousness. They were seemingly in the middle of nowhere when he heard her groan.

"Hey, how are you feeling?" Demolache said, gently slapping her face as she moaned and clutched her stomach. "Can you hear me?"

"I . . . I . . . It hurts."

"Okay, okay, just relax. Do you need food or water?"

"No . . . just let me sleep for a while."

Although still daylight, Demolache brought her over to a tree in the distance where he laid her down and got some rest himself.

INTERMISSION

"So you are capable of compassion?" I said, opening my eyes to Demolache sitting on the edge of my bed.

"I never said I wasn't," he whispered under his breath.

THE TREACHERY OF MAN

The next morning when Demolache woke, he found that Cat had finally made her recovery. She was examining her heart-shaped locket that hung from a silver chain around her neck. Her eyes cast a wish to the sky as she gripped the locket closed and let out a sigh.

"Good morning, you little delinquent. You were following me, weren't you?" Demolache sneered as he wiped the slumber from his eyes.

"Yes, I must get to the mountains where I can be free. That is the only place where I can feel free again. I figured since you were going as well, I should follow you." Cat spoke with her eyes still staring at the sky.

"Is that so? Remind me why that is? Who are you, Cat?" Demolache replied.

"I am nothing more than a wanderer like yourself. I left my village to find truth."

"Truth huh? Tell me your story. I'm willing to listen now," Demolache said, as he reached for an apple and some water.

Cat sat beside Demolache and took a large breath. "I was born as a companion to my older sister. She was the one whom my parents wanted, and she was cultivated for greatness. I was born to entertain her. After she had left the village, nothing I could do would impress them because my sister had achieved everything to perfection. I had no more purpose, and it filled me with so much rage. When I couldn't take it anymore, I acted out of envy and cursed my parents by burning the village to the ground," Cat said with a sigh, relieved to release her sin from her shoulders.

"Treachery!" Demolache screamed at this revelation. "You have acted against your own village out of envy, and now you seek freedom? What god would allow you to do such a thing?"

"Yes, I know what I did was wrong, but I did what I thought needed to be done! Erase my past to find freedom from my curse. I am godless like you! I have no purpose and seek one for my new life."

"How can I trust someone who is admittedly a heathen?" Demolache said and stormed off into the flat abyss.

Cat followed, screaming to him, "Demolache, Please stop! Please don't abandon me, we are the same now, aimless wanders with no past or future, searching for something to believe in!" She caught up to him, grabbing him by the arm and turning him to face her. "Don't leave me yet," she said, rising to the tips of her toes and touching her lips to his.

The kiss lasted about seven seconds before she returned her weight to her heels and Demolache, once again seduced by the touch of a woman, conceded to his more human side. "All right," he said, holding her by the hips and viewing her as a woman for the first time. "I shall bring you to the mountains where we will part ways and never see each other again," he stated with a sigh.

The entire trip took around fifty-eight days in total, and when they reached the peak of the mountains, Demolache was amazed by the world that lay before him. Through his eyes, I could see the whole world clearly. There were four levels to this world on which man existed. At the bottom, I saw a thick forest where people had to wander aimlessly, foraging for what food they could find while fending off wild beasts. On the next level were great cities in which people were dependent on each other for food and defense. The third level was full of rural farms in which people grew their own food and needed no protection, for they had chosen places where they could be content without threat. The very top, the last level of man's existence, was a mountain where people didn't need food or protection. They seemingly were fed and protected by God himself on those peaks. This was truly the happiest level of existence.

"I need to find God again. But first, I need to free myself from the beast that I have become. I'll never accept Him if I still have this rage," Demolache realized on that peak. He could not stay here. He had yet to complete his journey. To free himself of the pain was his new mission. So on the eve of his fifth day on the mountains, he told Cat, and she nodded.

"You told me we would part ways and so I have no resentment toward the idea, but I want you to take something with you," she whispered, as she removed the locket from around her neck and handed it to Demolache.

"Your locket? Your dearest possession?"

"Yes, take it with you and cherish it as I did."

"Thank you. I shall forever," Demolache said. The flames in his eyes began to extinguish ever so slightly as a glossy layer formed over them. "I must go now," he said with great sadness.

Trembling, Demolache gathered his things and began to descend the summit, heading west towards the cities. Every once in a while, however, he would stop and look back to see if Cat had followed him. He was disappointed that she hadn't. He hadn't forgotten about her sin, however, though he had put it to the back of his mind for the entire journey. Now that they were apart, he could finally begin to reconsider his judgment of her. She wasn't any different than the rest of the heathens he had come across. We were not one and the same for I am without sin, Demolache thought to himself for a moment. Am I though? Is it not sin to hold rage for those who are sinful? Does God not have wrath for heathens? Lost in thought, Demolache never realized that a mist had begun to envelop him, and within minutes he was swallowed by the fog.

SESSION III: THE MISERY

All I could think about today was Cat. In my memory, leaving her had been easy. It seemed different to Demolache. He hesitated and trembled. It also seemed like for a while there, he forgave her for her sins and never actually saw her as a monster. "Is she what you wanted?"

"You do not understand. I hesitated because Cat and Resh, although guilty of some of the worst sins, were still good people and I had trouble hating them. I wanted to save them. I wanted to help them somehow, but it was not my place to. They had already become monsters."

"Look at you, being all humane and what not. Where did that side of you go? What happened to the compassion of Demolache?"

Demolache's teeth tightened together and his fists clenched. "That is exactly what I am trying to show you."

DINING WITH SAVAGES

Demolache awoke a year later to find himself in a frozen wasteland. It was a desolate place where animals went to die. This was anything but a happy place, and yet the cry of people in the distance suggested otherwise. He picked himself up off the ground and started wandering in the direction of the voices. He eventually came to a small village full of what looked like savages. They were dancing around a fire, drinking and laughing. He hesitated at first but chose to interact with them anyway.

"Hello? Do you know where this is? Where are we?" Demolache casually interrupted.

The savages stopped their merriment and stared at Demolache. One stepped forward from the group with his shoulders held high. He glanced over at his men and then his impromptu village and then back to Demolache. He took a deep breath and then spoke.

"We . . . do not care."

The savages roared in laughter. They all began dancing again around the fire and drinking heavily from their jars. They were truly the happiest people Demolache had ever seen. The leader approached him with a jar. "Drink deeply and see the world through our eyes, for we don't drink because we want to, we drink because we have too."

Demolache took the jug and smelled the yellowish liquid inside. The smell stung his nostrils. "If this will truly make me happy, then I will indulge," Demolache said as he lifted the jug to his mouth. Though it tasted like piss, it sent volts of ecstasy through his body. His eyes enlarged, and his mind relaxed. Demolache took another gulp and another. He partied with the savages all night long.

INTERMISSION

"So that's your take on things?" I chuckled, still holding my eyes closed.

THE GLUTTONY AND THE RAGE OF MAN

The next morning, Demolache awoke to the worst pains he had ever felt. His head throbbed, and his stomach was in knots. He got up from the icy ground and saw the rest of the savages still sleeping. He tiptoed through the pack but was halted when he noticed that the leader was awake and waiting for him.

"Where are you off too?" the leader said with his arms crossed.

"I just don't feel good. I'm looking for food," he lied.

"Come with us, follow us, we are on our way west, to the cities. It is not something one can do easily alone."

Demolache agreed, somewhat regretfully, but for the next two months, he found himself having a decent time. They would all get food in the morning, walk all day, and then party all night. By the time they reached the cities, Demolache was a mess of his former self. He was constantly hung over and tired. He felt the same rage, but only towards himself. How could he let himself get so low? How could he fall in line with savages? He needed to continue his journey, and that thought would undo him.

As they entered the city in the middle of the night, two months after meeting the savages, he slipped away from the group and found his way to a church. Inside, he found a portly man garbed in monks robes, praying. Demolache's sudden entrance, as he was already intoxicated, drew the man's attention.

"My son, what is the meaning of this entrance in the middle of the night?" the robed man said.

"Fa'er, forgive . . . me, I'm sinner." He raised his hand as if to draw attention to himself. "Got no god or purpus in life. Help me back to the path. 'elp me find one. 'elp me find Him," Demolache demanded, slurring and spitting everywhere.

"My son, you may have left God, but God never left you. He is there for you whenever you are ready to receive Him back into your life," the man reasoned.

"But I don't actually want God, I want . . . His purpus, I want some'ing to believe in . . . for myself! Why do you believe? Why do you have God?" Demolache was screaming at this point. He fell on the floor promptly after finishing his sentence, out cold as if Bacchus had hit him over the head with a bottle.

A few hours later Demolache awoke, slightly more sober and definitely more coherent.

"Are you feeling better, my son?"

"What happened?" Demolache whispered, holding his head.

"You stumbled in here drunk and barely articulate. You then passed out on the floor," Edward replied. "The last thing you said to me was, 'Why do you believe?' Why would you ask me that?"

"Because I'm sad and alone in a hell of my own design," Demolache chuckled, holding his head, attempting to quell the pain that rattled within.

"I don't understand, my son. If you insist I can talk to you about my own personal journey, but first, tell me your name and why you are here in the middle of the night?"

"Okay . . . . I'm not really sure where to start, but I have spent the last two years of my life searching for answers and have found none. Lately, I have been drinking to forget about my journey but I cannot any longer. My name is Demolache. I'm looking for purpose, or something to believe in," Demolache said as he sat up in the bench next to the priest. "Now tell me how you found your purpose. Tell me how you decided on all of this."

"My son, my name is Edward, and I was like you, a savage who passively sought out truth. I was always told that God was truth, but I never truly understood that. Well . . . There was an incident a year ago, and I accepted the calling to help. I went to the people who had been hit by God's wrath, a storm which destroyed their lives. I went there because everyone else did; but after getting there, I saw what horror God had done to these people. It made me angry, and I wanted to kill myself for having more than them. I took a knife to my body, but before I struck, I heard God's calling. I was told that I was given as much as I was given in order to help these people. I saw that God had given me everything I had because he wanted me to serve Him. That is why I became a man of God. To help those whom God wanted me to help." Edward sat back in his seat and smiled, looking at the ceiling where images of Jesus's passion were elegantly drawn and painted.

Demolache also sat back in his seat at first, and then he stood up and turned to Edward. With his fist clenched and his teeth grinding he finally let out his damnation, "You pig!"

Edward was shocked at his reaction. "What did you say?"

"You follow God to justify your gluttony, you selfish pig!" Demolache bellowed throughout the church. He shoved Edward off the bench and ran out of the church, kicking things over and throwing Bibles across the room, knocking down a bowl that had inscribed inside of it: 'Piety to justify his appetite.' "Heathens! Is there no righteous man in this world?"

Demolache's rage set him afire, and he imagined his hands opening with the wounds of Christ. I, however, imagined that he grew a second set of upper canines. He began to run through the city as some sort of hulking beast, possessed with wrath, lighting it ablaze and throwing cars into buildings. People screamed as the rage of Demolache became inconsolable. He stomped cracks into the road and tore down whole buildings with his bare hands. He tore street lights out of concrete and whipped them around the city. Police cars surrounded him but they were no match for the monster within the man, and they were destroyed with little effort. For that period, he was the great white whale, cornered into ire. The city burned like his soul, the fires of a thousand ships invading against the Byzantines. The rage of Vesuvius erupted as the men and women watched—full of fear, full of guilt—the devastation and the horrors that were contained in his soul. Blue eyes burned with the pain of an abandoned child. When nothing else stood in his path of destruction, he screamed to the heavens while collapsing to his knees, "My God, my God, why have I abandoned you!"

The blue flames consumed him, and then everything went black.

INTERMISSION

"What?" Demolache demanded.

"Holy shit. What the fuck was that about?"

"I was upset."

"Fucking really? I don't exactly remember flipping cars and lighting a city on fire," I said, nervously, as I glanced over at the clock. Four a.m. again. I was so tired, but he just wouldn't let me sleep. I couldn't even react reasonably to the horror I had seen because I was apathetic when I was this tired.

"You hit bottom and lost control. That was my expression of your frustration, and it felt good," Demolache told me. "Now, I'm almost done the first part of my story. Just close your eyes."

FREEDOM'S COST

Demolache awoke to find that he was with the savages again. The leader was standing over him, kicking him in the side rather aggressively.

"You all right? You scared me back there, screaming about how you were Jesus and all. You. . . Destroyed that city like it was made out of blocks. It was . . . Kind of awesome."

"I'm fine, just lost my head for a little bit. I'm all good now."

"Come with me, I need to show you something."

Hung over and agitated, Demolache conceded and got up. Looking around, he saw that most of the other savages were still asleep. He was led through a small forest to a clearing with a cliff and a bridge.

"What is this?"

"This is the bridge to freedom. This is what you want, right? To be free from all of this? Just clear your mind and walk across. You will be freed from all worry and frustration if you can just let go and reach the other side," the leader said as he lit his cigarette.

It was an old wooden tie bridge, and its destination was blocked by a thick cloud of mist. What had Wood said about the mist? We could never see the other side? Demolache took a deep breath and gripped the rope tie of the bridge. He took a few steps as a storm brewed overhead. It began to rain, and a fierce wind picked up. He took a few more steps and then he paused.

"We are the gods of our existence. Just let go of all of your rage, let go of your hate. It's the only thing tethering you to this hell hole of a world," a voice called from behind him.

He stood on the rope bridge that lay before him. The high winds and rain seemed to have held him back, but he stepped forward anyway. Was this the end of his journey? The answer that he was looking for? As he walked, he could feel the tension within the jagged ropes, yet he maintained a steady pace as he made his way across. The destination was still unknown as a thick fog covered the island on the other side. Further across, the wind and rain began to intensify gradually until this body started to give in to the intense weight. The bridge began to sway violently, but instead of holding tighter, he bowed his head to protect his eyes from the rain that pelted this body like bullets. As if the island had roared, the wind thrashed out down the length of the bridge and threw him from his feet. His head hit first, slamming into the wooden cross bars as if he were a smooth rock being cast into the ocean and he began to bleed heavily. Remaining there for a moment, I thought back to those he had encountered along the way. Wood, the greedy fisherman. Rin the lustful beast of the oasis. Khat, the proud doctor. Resh, the slothful noble. The treacherous wanderer Cat. Edward, the gluttonous priest. They were all heathens who had found a purpose for their lives by unjustifiable means. They were monsters. So was I better than them? I thought to myself. Was I without sin? He slammed his fist onto the wooden boards and lifted himself, only to lash out. "I don't fear you anymore," he bellowed to the mist and began to run across the bridge at full speed. The wind and rain became as intense as ever, but he seemed unaffected. "I am not the puppet of some false ideal, I have nothing to believe in." Three-fourths of the way down the length of the bridge, Demolache stopped. The rain had stopped. The wind had stopped. The sun had appeared, and with it, a feeble figure emerged from the end of the bridge.

"Demolache," the figure called to him is a soft voice.

"What is this nonsense?"

"Demolache, don't do this," the figure called to him again.

"What is the meaning of this, stranger?" Demolache bellowed in a fit of rage.

"If you truly were ready, then you wouldn't still blame yourself for his death, you wouldn't still hold such contempt for everything imperfect in this world. You have to have hope." And with that, the figure disappeared, and the rain and wind returned instantly and harder than ever.

I collapsed under the pressure of Demolache's wrath. Was it me he was angry at? Or was it his God whom he had abandoned? Either way, the rage consumed him as he let go a terrifying cry. Just then, he was struck by a bolt of rogue lighting and flung from the bridge into the briny deep. As water filled his lungs, we thought back to the beginning of his journey. Where did I go wrong? The locket around his neck began to float, and for the first time Demolache reached for it and opened it.

The locket had written inside, "In her envy, she acted out of frustration, treachery in an attempt for love." Demolache ripped the chain off his neck and flung it through the water in frustration. He didn't see it, but I did. Most people don't sin for the sake of evil, but you can't see that Demolache. You only see people as monsters.

Part Two: The Fight
2.5 years ago

SESSION IV: THE COUNCILS

PREMONITION TWO

"Demolache! Do not blame yourself for this!" The woman cried out, her voice jarred by the rhythm of the beast's stride as he carried her off into the setting sun like a robber with the loot of his career. The knives on his back scraped and cut her flesh, but she barely fought for her freedom. She barely fought at all.

"No! I will not let this happen!" screamed an enraged Demolache, full stride behind them. Feet like the hooves of a mad horse, charging for glory. His body had become a machine, pumping adrenaline like fuel into the combustion engine of his eight cylinder heart. "I won't let them take you!" One by one he threw down the pieces of his armor in order to gain more speed, his chest plate, and shoulders, his helm and boots, and when it wasn't enough, he even cast aside his swords as he chased the beast through the woods of purgatory.

He chased them till midnight, neither letting up for even the slightest bit of breath. They had run as far as they could go and when there was nowhere else to run, the chase ended at a dock that led off into a sea of clouds.

"Let her go!" he screamed, brandishing his fists and clenching his teeth. The journey had only made his engine stronger. He was not tired. It took all the self-control he could muster not to tear the beast down with the girl on its shoulder, but he knew that she needed to be safe before he could release all of God's judgment on the two-headed monster. "It's me you want. Let her go. Let's settle this between us. What is your name?"

But this demon knew not to speak its name. "I am the beast of a thousand names and to reveal one would only serve to dishonor my namesake," one of its heads said. "So let's make a deal. We can skip these formalities, and I'll give you what you want if you give me what I want," the other said after.

"I don't make deals with devils, heathen. I want the girl, and then we can talk, on the field of battle," Demolache crackled. He could barely speak over the rage that was building.

"Relax, all we want is the necklace."

"Yeah, give me the necklace, and I will give you the girl. We will even shake on it," the demon said. Little did Demolache know who he was dealing with.

The necklace he was referring to was Cat's locket, which was still around his neck despite the events of the last two years. The whole thing confused him. Why the necklace? Of all things, was this what they were all after? Just a stupid locket? "Why do you want this?" he said, removing the necklace from his body.

"Well you see . . ." the demon's heads took turns saying, extending his hand and retrieving the silver locket. "After you killed my brothers, I had a great idea . . ." He held the locket to the sky and then grinned his devilish grin on both faces. "To take any hope you have left . . ." One head's eyes dropped to meet with Demolache's. "And simply throw it away!" the demon bellowed out, and as careless and whimsical as a child casting a wish into the night sky, in one fluid motion, he threw everything Demolache held dear in this world into the pits below.

Everything happened in slow motion as Demolache shoved the demon aside and struggled to untie a rope from the side of the dock. As he did so and re-tied it into a lasso, he saw the girl floating before his very eyes. She was an angel gracefully gliding through the air, her hair blowing in the wind and her arms open wide. Gravity was a lie for those seconds. Right before time sped up again, she said these words:

"Oh Demolache, worry not. I will be back for you one day."

And then she fell . . .

INTRODUCTION

Demolache's story had been having a terrible effect on my life. The last three days I had been so tired and cranky that I had just been angry at everyone. This must have been how he felt. Constantly angry and pointing out other people's flaws. What I didn't understand is how one-sided he could be. Even in his own story, all the characters so far had redeeming qualities. Wood was content with a devout life. Rin was happy living in the present and really wasn't that different than a lot of people. Khat was allowed to be proud of his religion. Resh had compromised his knowledge and spiritual needs into one philosophy. Cat had been much happier without the pressure of her sister's shadow. Edward had repurposed his life so that he could help people. Everyone was just trying to make their lives better. So what if they were guilty of sin? Was there no merit in sin as a means to virtue? Not in Demolache's eyes. His wrath had no end. The worst offender of vice should be himself since he wasn't even accomplishing anything by means of his wrath. I let out a great sigh and drank deep from a bottle of whiskey that I now kept beside my bed. It made this whole experience go down a little more smoothly.

"Oh great. You brought an old friend," Demolache cackled, referring to the bottle in my hand. "Does that mean you're ready to continue? This is my favorite part, after all. The part where I escaped the pit and became a hero." Demolache smirked as he appeared out of nowhere.

"I know. I'm curious to see exactly how that happened. There was no more sleep for me after that point in my life."

"I merely woke up a better man, but I owe everything to those who let me live."

PAST, PRESENT, AND FUTURE

Everything grew blacker and blacker as the man fell into deeper and deeper desperation. He reached out but could not grasp anything, not even himself. He was completely intangible and his screams inaudible. The speed of his fall was slowly damped as his fading became final. At his wits' end, however, was when he saw a hand, glossed in white light, reach out to him. He reached back, but upon touching it was met with a grave pain.

Demolache awoke, coughing violently as salt water spewed out of his mouth. After catching his breath, he realized he was on a boat with an old owl-like man pressing on his chest.

"This boy is awake," the creature said, turning to the other two owl-men who nodded as they continued to row.

Demolache sat up in a fright to see he was on a small row boat that seemed to be going in circles. "Where am I? Who are you?" he said, startled at the three staring at him. Was this another dream? Certainly there were not actually three owls in a boat simply roaming the ocean and rescuing lost souls. This whole thing seemed so fucked up. "Wake up, wake up," he whispered to himself silently.

The younger owl who was paddling on the right side of the boat was the first to respond. "We will not be very good at answering your questions clearly."

The oldest owl then replied, "You had a terrible fall. You almost drowned in those waters. We saved you." He was paddling on the left side in a counter-intuitive backward motion. The combination of the two paddling made the boat spin in small circles in the water. If the boat had been going any faster, it would have made Demolache very dizzy.

The middle-aged owl man who had returned to the front of the craft then spoke. "We are here to help you, if you want our help. Otherwise, you are free to return to the water." He then handed Demolache a canteen.

Demolache drank deeply from the seemingly bottomless bottle until the taste of fish pee and salt were rinsed from his pallet. He had hoped the dehydration was just making him delirious, but to his disappointment, the owls were still there when he was finished. "Thank you, I guess, but how did you find me? And how can you help me?"

"You had lost this in the water. We retrieved it." The oldest owl reached under his seat to reveal the silver locket that Cat had given him.

He grabbed the locket and after a moment of hesitation hung it around his neck, tucking it under his shirt. Wait. Where had he gotten this shirt from? "Thanks . . . that's not all you want to help me with . . . is it?"

The two stopped rowing, and all three stared through Demolache. The experience was horrifying.

"We are taking you where you need to go. If you are willing to go."

"We will be there shortly if you will answer our one question."

"We knew who you were, Demolache, what you had done."

"We want to know who you will become. What will be your fate?"

"So who are you? What are you?"

Demolache trembled. He felt like he was being judged. One wrong word and he would be back in the water. "I don't know . . ." he managed to say after a long pause. "I don't know who I am . . ."

"That was your problem, in my opinion."

"It is a problem that a man your age cannot answer such a simple question."

"It will be your demise if you don't find an answer."

"I am sorry, I am trying my best to think, but all I know is that I am a wanderer," Demolache replied.

"You were a demon."

"You are lost."

"You will die."

"I am sorry it's just . . ." Demolache hesitated for a moment. "It's just that you call me by a name that I truly don't even know if it is mine," Demolache screamed.

The three cocked their heads in confusion. As if to ask, "What?" Yet none of them spoke. They just looked at each other in confusion. He had their full attention now.

Demolache took a deep breath and just let it all out. "For two years I have searched for the answer to such questions, but it seems like all I have answered is the question of what instead of who. I am a monster. I am many monsters, for I bear the sins of all I have met heavy in my heart. To them, I have provided the service of taking on their stories to free them of their burdens. But what did I gain from this? How do I feel?" Demolache began to cry. "More lost. More pain. More angry at a world that allows such heathens to roam free. I can't even call them heathens because I am not free of sin myself. Yes, I am guilty of wrath. Yes, I tried to free myself from my sins. I have acted recklessly against my fellow man, but I did all this and more in the pursuit of truth! That truth I seek is an answer to the question, who am I? And what is my purpose? Please do not leave me in these waters and do not bring me back to that hell without giving me a chance at some greater purpose. Please let me pursue something meaningful! I beg this of you! And if you don't, then give me death. I am a man betrayed by God and abandoned by my grandfather, just looking for something to believe in."

The bird-men were silent for a little while as Demolache continued to sob something desperate on the floor of the boat. It was like all of the pain and sorrow that he had masked with anger had suddenly burst out in one heartfelt speech. It was beautiful, watching him finally accept his misery instead of burying it down deep. It felt . . . liberating . . .

The owls turned to each other in a huddle. They began debating what had been said, what to say, and what they would do.

"He has admitted his crimes."

"And now is begging for another chance."

"What will we do?"

"We are to be merciful."

"Will it not just end the same?"

"Have you some new idea?"

"He is our lure."

"Yes . . . Perhaps he will chase the fox out of his hole."

"We have been wrong before. What about this has convinced you?"

"His intervening is already proof enough."

They looked at the boy and then back to each other.

"I don't think it will work, but it will be fun to watch."

"I had thought this was simple, but now what other choices have we?"

"Then we are in agreement?"

"Yes," the younger and older conceded.

"Good. Purgatory it is."

The three conspirators turned to Demolache again, who was only now pulling himself off the floor. "Why are you looking at me like that?"

The three giggled and smiled. They spoke in unison as their heads seemingly merged, only a few words were off, "You [have/are having/will have] one chance. If you [had failed/fail/will fail] to find happiness, this illusion [crumbled/crumbles/will crumble]. Off to purgatory you [had gone/will go/are going]. So [had said/says/will say] the fates."

"What?" Demolache whimpered back.

The waters turned turbulent as the laughter of the owls faded along with their image. All around the boat, the waters rose to form great walls. The boat was sinking into a large depression in the water, and the sky turned pale white. Without warning, the water invaded the depression causing a huge upward surge that sent the boat, and Demolache of course, into the air. His faint scream could be heard throughout hell like the first lead at Lexington. In a far off land, a blue-sheathed man looked into the sky with great fear . . .

PURGATORY

Purgatory. Demolache had been living in hell for the first two and a half years of his life. That's how he saw it, at least. This was a new opportunity for him. A chance for him to let go of his rage and just be happy. Being content with his existence seemed easy enough. However, there were others who wished to see him fail. There were those who wanted to see him prevail also, but the prior would be satisfied first. It was a war of the hearts and a divine beauty contest for different ways to live. This Paris, however, would leave without a Helen. So had decided the fates.

Demolache awoke in the outer forests of a small island. He was relieved to discover that he was alone. No stabbing spears or over-watching doctors. No bird-like revivals or aggressive kicks. It brought a smile to his face. Upon standing, he felt light as a feather. "What is this place?" he remarked, as he soon realized that the island literally sat upon a sea of clouds. It was beautiful. Like seeing Rome for the first time after living in a sewer. This was the exalted capital of something great.

He then turned his attention to a dense forest where he began exploring. In sharp contrast to where he had spent the last two and a half years, there was a mystical element to the flora and fauna. They seemed to have more texture, more weight to them. They seemed more . . . real. He explored further, noticing that far fewer trees bore fruit and on those that did the fruit was out of reach or defended by thick and thorny vines. Purgatory was truly a place of wondrous juxtapositions. Everything had a positive and a negative element. It was beautiful how great a change of perspective could affect his environment. If only it weren't all a lie.

Attracted by the sound of running water, Demolache made his way to a nearby river, where he saw an astonishing sight. It appeared to be a woman with blue skin, blowing smoke. She sat at the river's edge, simply enjoying existence. He approached with great hesitation and hid behind a tree, mesmerized by the draw and blow back of the smoke.

"Do you want a cigarette or are you going to just be creepy?" She broke the silence when she noticed him. She spoke with such apathy, such disdain, it filled him with a deep sense of hopelessness. The mystical first moments in purgatory were ruined by a few words.

"Why do you smoke? Isn't that poison? Don't those kill you?"

"Yeah, well, we are all dying, so pick your poison," she retorted with a chuckle.

Demolache approached her and sat at the water's edge. He took a cigarette and, after careful examination, lit it. It burned his insides as he inhaled, but it filled him with a strange calm. He exhaled through his nose and watched the deadly smoke dance around his head. There were two things that seduced Demolache: woman and death. The latter is what drove Demolache to begin smoking. Something about killing himself made him remember his origin. It made him feel needed again. It was his goal to keep me alive, and the chance of this new found habit killing him slowly gave him a sense of purpose again: to kill me so that I needed him to survive. What an asshole.

After a moment of silence, he finally asked the question that had been on the tip of his tongue. "Where am I?"

She sighed something sad. "Purgatory. Little bit of heaven, little bit of hell. It's all the same to me," she chuckled.

Demolache began looking around and then smiled with an equal sigh. "Can you show me around? I'm kinda new here . . ."

Tor rolled her eyes. "Fine," she replied, tossing her lit cigarette into the clear and shimmering waters. It made Demolache weep inside.

Tor led him to a city within the island where he saw monsters living in peace. Well . . . Sort of. They were all half monsters. Nothing like what he had seen in hell, just ordinary people with imperfection. There were people with claws, people with fangs, people with scales on their skin, people with scars, some healed and some still bleeding, They looked like ordinary people but to Demolache, each had its flaw. This was the phaneron he had developed in hell after all. To see the sin in others. Their vices as opposed to their virtues. She showed him to a small eight-by-ten room where he would spend most of the next few months of his life. It wasn't much, but it would be a home. She helped him set up a bed, a desk, and even a T.V. so that Demolache would be able to relax and indulge his habit of staying up all night trying to understand his predicament and where he was to go from here. As he would discover soon, it failed to suppress his hunger.

On one particular evening, increasingly discontent with mediocrity, Demolache stood outside his humble cage staring at the night sky and smoking his cigarette when through the abyss came a moth. Attracted to the light outside his home, it fluttered and danced about, refusing to land but unwilling to give up. He thought deeply about the moth's predicament. We have come so far as a species. Always moving forward and never looking back. We have destroyed whole ecosystems in pursuit of something that we don't even know is there. What did moths do before electricity? Did they chase the sun? Did they chase fires? Where did this hunger for light come from? Perhaps they don't run toward the light, perhaps they run from something. Darkness. They fear the abyss. They fear not knowing what stalks the night behind them.

Demolache approached the light slowly and stretched out his arm. To his amazement, the moth danced around his arm but refused to land on him. "Still angry?" he said to the moth, who did nothing in reply. "I know," he whispered still transfixed on its flight. "I know I can't stay."

Demolache stomped out his cigarette and ran back inside to grab a jacket. He was going to run away from this stalemate his life had become. He needed to find purpose instead of just sitting around all day inside his head. He ran through the streets of the city to find his way back to the forest, and not until he reached it did he finally slow down. The majority of the island was made up of forests and mountains. He could still have an adventure like he did in hell. He could still find people's answers to feed off of. Monsters to judge. And so he wandered those woods looking for just that—a monster.

It wasn't long before Demolache came across a small man writing in the woods. He was a lotus eater named Zel who was writing poetry. This short Irishman was garbed in strange colors and seemed to care little for social norms. Only doing what he needed to get by. Truly a waste, in Demolache's opinion. A good catch for a monster hunter, he giggled to himself. He crept towards the man, cigarette in hand.

"What are you doing here? Writing?" Demolache whispered, approaching the man from behind.

Zel jumped, startled by the approach, tossing papers into the air. "Je'sus Christ, ya scared the fuck right out of me, ya did!" he screamed as the papers began to settle on the ground. "It's . . . po'try . . . ya know, words from the hart instead of the mind."

Demolache was amused at having disturbed and upset the man. "Poetry huh? Are you any good?"

Zel was still noticeably annoyed at Demolache, but he was quickly overcome by a sense of pride that someone might want to read his work. "Ya want to read some'ing?"

Demolache took the tattered notebook and began skimming the lines as Zel lit a cigar of his own. The lyrics that decorated the page spoke of deep sadness and darkness. It was the passion and pain in dichotomized verse of a man who found himself cast aside by fate and love.

"Not bad, it's a bit dark though . . . Why do you write with such sadness?" Demolache asked, returning the notebook.

Zel took a deep breath before offering his soul for judgment. "I was bred a military man. Me father believed it the only good thin' for 'is oldest son." Zel let out another sigh. "So when I was the age to join the mil'tary, I gave it me all, I really worked bloody hard. It wasn't enough thoh . . . I was rejected 'ventually. Not army material, they said. Didn't know where else to go with me life. Was a reject of me fate. Had a womon too, beautiful 'ittle flower she was. She, too, rejected me soon after. Said I changed. I gave up me dreams and me love. Said fuck it. Moved to this forest. Write me poetry to ease the pain and sadness. Trap it inside of somethin' other than meself."

Demolache inhaled deep and then released his smoke. "So you're a reject of fate. Interesting." He began walking back and forth in thought. I knew what he wanted to say. Demolache hadn't changed. Sloth. Envy. Content with a meaningless existence just like Resh. He hadn't escaped the demons that surrounded him. Nothing had changed. He took a deep breath and finally spoke, "Do you really believe you can trap a part of yourself by words alone?"

After a moment's thought, Zel responded with a furrowed brow, "Ya can do anythin' if you believe hard enough."

This bothered Demolache for some reason. As if his words were a spear, hurled through his heart by Diomedes himself. "Lying to yourself is not the same as changing reality. Get a job." Demolache put out his cigarette. He simply walked away instead of letting loose his full wrath. He could have destroyed that man. Given him something to really write about. He didn't, though. Had he changed? Probably not. Maybe his response had thrown him off guard, alluded to a truth he didn't want to accept. Or maybe it was just too easy. This wasn't a man who had chosen a path or believed in anything. He had just given up. A meaningless existence. Kind of like how Demolache felt right now. It made him happy in a sick way to know that there were still demons here, despite how different this place was, yet he couldn't shake an eerie feeling he had gotten from that conversation.

"Thank ya mister!" Zel screamed from behind.

Demolache's face contorted but he didn't turn around. "For what?" he said.

"I din know, understandin' I guess," Zel stuttered out.

Demolache closed his eyes and continued walking. He smiled for a moment, and then it faded.

Demolache doesn't understand you, I thought to myself, he hates you. He hates you for accepting your imperfections and shortcomings. It was a hatred that I was ashamed of and it brought pain to my very soul. However, it made what happened next all the more satisfying for me to watch. Demolache had only walked maybe forty feet before a paper bag was thrown over his head and a bottle smashed on his left temple. He was dragged away into the night . . .

INTERMISSION

"Yeah, something like that . . ." I said, with my eyes still shut tight and a grin from ear to ear.

There was a chuckle somewhere in the room. Or was it in my head? I still don't understand this dynamic, which is sad considering that I'm writing in hindsight. I let out a great sigh and then returned to the story.

TOR'S WARNING

When the bag was removed from Demolache's head, he found himself back home in his room. Tor was the one holding the bag. She didn't say anything at first. She just paced back and forth. He felt as though he were in trouble for some reason.

Tor finally turned to him. "You can't just go wandering the woods in the middle of the night. You could have gotten hurt. You could have died. There are terrible things out there. Things you don't want to encounter."

Demolache's fist clenched, and he ground his teeth. "Why do you care what happens to me? What I see? If I chose to pursue this path, then the decision is mine alone!"

"You're right, why should I even bother?" she said, grabbing her coat and heading for the door.

"Wait!" Demolache screamed after her. "What is out there? Why should I be afraid?"

Tor paused at the door. "There is nothing worth searching for out there. You have a home here. Be content with that much. Don't go chasing something you don't want to find." With that, she left.

Don't go searching for what? Meaning? Purpose? Why wouldn't I want to find it? Demolache thought to himself.

"Because," Tor's voice entered my head, "They will find you."

Who will find me? What is she trying to protect me from? Demolache drifted off to sleep. Accepting his meaningless life, for the moment, and possibly appeasing his concussion.

THE ESCAPE

His eyes opened. They stared at a point that I could not see. The detail of the room came into focus. Our body was numb. No movement. No voice. I was at peace, and my mind was adrift. Shadows danced in contrast against white walls. Ambient sounds were soothing. His mind had never produced such detail: color; sounds; touch. It was all so real. Wait. No. I was conscious. This was no dream. Awaken. Move. Move, dammit, move!

He was soon seized by fear. He commanded but received no response. Catatonic consciousness. Paranormal paralysis.

He was trapped. His heart beat in violent variations. His nose began to bleed. Panic personified. Fear unfettering. Move, please move!

His thoughts grew loud, but his heart beat louder. He screamed, and then the hold released. His body recoiled into a ball. His breath was uncontrollable. What had just happened? Sleep so deep no more. He would not attempt sleep again tonight.

It had been weeks since his first attempt at escape and Demolache had tried to accept this awful fate. He felt caged and controlled. Used and underutilized. This dream he kept having . . . Or maybe it wasn't dream? He would wake first in his mind and then in his body, causing fits of panic on a grand scale. The dreams stole his ability to sleep and caused his nose to burst blood. His pillow had become the shroud of Turin, a silhouette of his sacrifice drawn in blood. He needed to do something. Escape! His heart screamed in staggered beats. And so he tried one last time. He waited until the middle of the night, grabbing his supplies and then booking it back into the forest, turning his back on the reality of his new life.

It wasn't long before he saw a familiar face standing at the edge of the woods. Tor. She had brought a friend. His name was Ret; a tall, beaked man who wore a suit.

"Just let me go," Demolache shouted at the two. He felt defeated by their presence. As if they had predicted this. Olympus had intervened, and swift Hermes had not been beat, winged-shoed jerk.

The two figures looked at each other and then at Demolache.

"We might. Just answer us this one question. Why?" Ret said, standing with his arms crossed.

"What do you mean, why? Why should you let me go?" Demolache returned.

Tor sighed. "No, why is this so important to you? Why do you need to find some sort of purpose? Why can't you be content with who you are? With what you are?"

Demolache didn't know how to respond. He had never even asked himself these questions. "Well," he managed to say. "I'm afraid."

The two looked at each other again, then back at Demolache.

"I need to keep searching. I have to find something. A reason to wake up in the morning. A purpose that can guide my life. I fear that if I don't find something I don't know what I will become. I'm so angry. I'm so discontent with this. With everything this is. I feel like . . ."

"A god that has been shackled?" Tor sighed again. "Fine. Go. But don't expect us to pick up the pieces if you fall again . . ."

Demolache smiled. "Thanks," he whispered.

"For what?" she replied sarcastically.

"For understanding," Demolache smirked as he ran full force into the woods.

Ret turned to watch as Demolache disappeared out of view. "You know we are going to have to follow him."

"Just let him do his thing for now."

"He's dangerous."

"Just a bit neurotic."

"We'll watch over him."

"Fine. Just to make sure."

FORBIDDEN FRUIT

Demolache wandered the woods of purgatory for days. He was hungry, thirsty, and tired. More than anything he was afraid. What could possibly lurk in the woods that would scare Tor, of all people? The images of Cyclops and Centaurs entered his mind, deceiving him into a state of paranoia. He was not in good shape. How long could he continue? How long before he would become—

"Deliriouthhh?" a voice lisped out.

"Who said that! Who is there?" Demolache whirled around to search his surroundings. Nothing. But his head was pounding. He was dizzy and confused.

"Why tho angry Demolache?" the serpent said, as it began to slither out of Demolache's nose.

"What devil play is this!" In a panic, Demolache ripped the snake out of his nose and threw it upon the ground. It curled and recoiled to gain its bearing and then lurched its head up to face him.

"Relaxth great warrior, I am here to help you. To guide you," it hissed out.

"Where did you come from? What are you?" Demolache asked as he got down to examine the snake at eye level.

"I came from inthide you. Inthide your very thoul. Follow me if you want your anthers," the snake hissed as it made its way across the floor of the forest.

"This is fucked, I have to be hallucinating. Maybe I'm still asleep? Hopefully, I'll wake soon."

"You will, trutht me. You are about to wake up in more wayth than one," the snake hissed back. "Tell me, are you thick of being tho angry all the time? How far would you go jutht to have a purpoth?"

A stumbling and delirious Demolache was in no position to think clearly. "Anything. I would do anything,"

Demolache screamed out. "I'm sick of this rage, I'm sick of hating everyone I have ever met!"

"Then eat!" The snake spoke as it slithered up a tree and knocked loose a fruit from the top. "Eat, Demolache, and let it thooth your thoul. I will thow you a man without thin," the snake chuckled.

A starved Demolache ran up to the fruit and began devouring it. With every bite, his body felt lighter and lighter. Before he could even finish, he let out a happy little grin and then fell backward. Unconscious . . .

"Fucking athhhole," a voice could be heard trailing off.

THE OBSERVERS' COMMENT

"This is what I was afraid of. You idiot, Demolache."

"You can't blame him. Everyone who enters this forest populates it with their own demons. Just be glad he only had one. It takes a very strong man to navigate here. A man who knows himself would have little problem."

"Hopefully he wakes up as that man," Tor chuckled.

"Hopefully he won't continue to reject reality."

"Let's bring him to the river. At least he'll wake up with water."

UTNAPISHTIM THE LEGENDARY

Demolache "woke" on a great beach. Grey water. Grey sand. Grey sky. He went to the water's edge to drink, but the water burned his skin as he attempted to cup it into his mouth. "What the hell is this place?"

"He is waiting for you," a deep voice bellowed out as something broke the surface of the water and approached Demolache.

Demolache jumped at the sight of the massive gray monster. Its body was emaciated skin on bone, and its face was a permanent frown carved into tree bark. There were sockets where eyeballs should have been and spindly dead branches for hair.

"What the fuck are you!" Demolache screamed out to the giant.

Without moving its mouth, the monster spoke in its booming pitch. "I am the ferryman. Servant of the chosen one. The great Utnapishtim awaits." It reached out its great cupped hands for Demolache to step upon.

A cautious Demolache stepped into its clutches, and the creature began walking back out into the corrosive waters. What the fuck was going on? He thought to himself.

As they got closer and closer to their destination, the ferryman sank deeper and deeper into the gray waters below, lifting Demolache further into the sky with one hand. It wasn't until the island in the distance was visible that the monster started to emerge again from the depths. He placed Demolache on the island and spoke. "Twelve hours, Demolache. If you are not ready to go then, I will leave you here forever." The enigma spoke as it leaned backward. Back into the depths like a large tower slowly losing its fight to gravity, it angled farther and faster into a parallel position, finally causing a great splash.

Demolache shuddered and walked towards a small cottage on the island, the only feature the island had to offer. It was a gray house with gray grass and gray smoke billowing out the top. He knocked on the door, anticipating the worst. The man who answered was named John.

John seemed to be the most pious of the outcasts Demolache had met since coming to purgatory. It was hard to believe that he had previously been a demon. The journey to find him was strange, to say the least, but to find a man of God that was free from all sin was definitely worth it.

"For what purpose do I deserve this visit?" John laughed, answering the door.

"My name is Demolache. I am a man without purpose, searching for something to sooth my angry thoul."

"Well, that sounds familiar." John laughed again, like Saint Nicholas in the summertime; it was hard to imagine a more jolly man. "I must ask, however, how did you end up here? I haven't had a visitor since Gilgamesh himself did attempt to cheat death."

Demolache paused, thinking back. "I don't know. I woke up on that beach and then the ferryman carried me over here. There was a snake too. He promised me I would find answers here. I don't think he was a good person though. He seemed kinda like a jerk."

John looked at him with great confusion. "Well . . . I um . . . I can't promise you answers . . . Or understand what any of that means. I am simply a man of God and know only His grace and His glory. What you seek seems beyond my power."

Demolache was angered by his response. "How can you believe in an intangible deity? Your only proof is a two-thousand-year-old manuscript that has been translated so many times, who knows what they were originally describing?"

The pious John, however, was unflinching in his demeanor. "It's just like how you know the earth is round. You haven't seen it or measured it, but you believe it to be true beyond a reasonable doubt."

"Yes, but people have proved that time and time again, and if I wanted to test it, then I would find the same result. The two are not equal," Demolache retorted.

"Aristotle has an answer for you there but let's not get metaphysical. How about this . . . How do you know you are alive?"

Demolache paused for a while and thought. "I just know I am. I can look at my hand. I can feel my consciousness."

"Exactly. In the same way, I know that God exists because I can look around at all the beauty in the world and see that something had to have created it," John said with confidence.

Demolache was baffled by this. Beauty. He had little experience with the concept. All he knew was imperfection. Flaws. Sins. Vice. Demons. Monsters. Betrayal. Abandonment. There was no beauty in any of it. Before he could respond there was a bell from the oven.

"You're just in time for dinner," John said, leaping into his kitchen and removing a tray from the oven. It was an array of vegetables surrounding a roasted lamb. The smell was one thing, but the taste was amazing. Greater than anything he had ever tasted in his short life. "My wife put this together, no need to thank me," he chuckled.

Stop being so fucking happy and humble, Demolache thought to himself with slight resentment.

INTERMISSION

At this point, I just needed to stretch and remove myself from this insanity. "This story gets more and more ridiculous every night, Demolache."

"All that matters is that you see where I came from. Understand what happened to lead us to this point."

"I'm just glad you got one person right. Saw what I saw for once."

"I was a fool to trust him. He gave me no answers, he just helped me pacify my rage. It only made things worse."

"I know," I said with a melancholy sigh. That pain. I can't. Not now. It was too much to bear.

THE HOPE OF DEMOLACHE

John explained that he didn't ever need to leave the island to gather food; rather, God provided all he needed. John explained a lot of things and by the time the meal was finished the two had become good friends. Shortly after, Demolache realized what he really wanted to ask John. The question on the tip of his tongue was never what, but rather why.

"So what's your story then, why do you believe?" Demolache said, after noticing his time was running short.

"Is that really important?"

"For someone like me who has lost their way, it is important that I figure out how to get it back. Demolache's head dropped slightly. There was a shame in his godlessness. As if he were sheathed from God's light for so long that its sudden appearance was blinding and repulsive. He had felt it first when Khat diagnosed him so quickly. Khat. Maybe it was my fault that he got so defensive. I couldn't take my words back. I could never take back what I had done.

John sighed deeply. "Alright, if you must know. I was once in love with a beautiful woman back when I was like you. We spent so much time together, inseparable like the sky and the seas."

"A woman turned you to God? That seems backward."

John shook his head and continued. "One day, she was involved in a horrible accident. She was hurt badly and couldn't remember who she was, let alone who I was. It was devastating for the woman you love to just not remember who you are one day. I stayed by her side until she made her recovery. The day she did, she left me. The pain filled me until it was unbearable. I was thrown into a world of darkness until one day I resolved to end it once and for all. I was mere seconds away from taking my own life when I felt something beside me. It was the most beautiful of flowers that had seemingly sprung up just to remind me that my life was worth living. I believe it was sent by God himself. For this, I will never doubt his existence. That flower saved my life and brought me back into the light. His light. This is why I believe."

Demolache was angered by this. Could a man truly without sin even exist? The idea brought him so much pain and sadness that he couldn't speak. It was as if this story had put out the fires in his soul like a great rain. Could he be saved in such a manner? Was he, too, not a lost cause? Could he be redeemed by something as simple as a flower? He was brought back to life by this idea. He was inspired to make this his new meaning. He needed to find a flower to make him see God. He needed to find something so beautiful that he had no choice but to reach the conclusion that there was a conscious and caring God. He no longer wanted this rage, this anger in his soul.

He left with the ferryman soon afterward, still lost in thought.

BORN AGAIN

Demolache came to several hours later with his head halfway in a stream of water. Was it all a hallucination? He quickly drank and washed off his face. Had he never left the woods? Was any of it real? He needed to clear his head for a moment. He was overwhelmed by the things he thought he had heard. The revelations he thought he had received. Could it be that easy? He undressed and entered the water. It was cold to the touch but refreshing to the senses. It was as if all worry and caution eroded into the stream and all that was left was a sculpture created by his environment like the rocks beneath his feet. The water was so clear. So clear, in fact, that something at the bottom of the river caught his eye. He swam down to approach it, and to his surprise, it was a blue water lily, sank to the bottom of Ea's ocean. He reached out to the flower, its petals so alluring and colorful. It moved the way a nude woman moves to taunt onlookers with her beauty. Like a siren of the Ionian, she pulled his wayward soul towards—fuck! Demolache thought as the pain began jolting up and down his arms. This flower had thorns. Volatile ones. The neurotoxin paralyzed his body. He began floating downstream, unable to swim against the current. His body surfaced just in time to see the crash and roar of the rapids ahead. "Shit!" he screamed, closing his eyes tight.

He crashed into the pond below with great force, scraping on rocks and rolling around in the surf. Washing up on the edge of the pond, he lay unmoving for a while before opening his eyes. Twitching about, he let out a great smile and an even greater laugh. His hair matted, covered with a thin layer of blood, he was like a newborn; nude and unconditionally happy. He took his first breath of this new life he had entered into and let out another laugh. Cold breeze between his legs, he set out back to the city, full sprint and full of . . . vigor . . .

"Umm . . ." a disturbed onlooker commented.

"I wish I could unsee that."

"Should we be worried?"

Ret looked at Tor with a sarcastic grin "Nah, this is completely normal behavior."

INTERMISSION

I was unable to keep myself from laughing loudly in the loneliness of my room.

"What?" Demolache replied, attempting to stop himself from laughing as well.

"Nothing." I thought back to the memory he was drawing upon with a large smile. "So then what?"

THE BULL OF HEAVEN

Demolache, now clothed after his streaking episode through the city streets, geared up for one last adventure. He was going hunting for a flower—or a woman rather—a woman that would be worth his self-value and allow him to see the beauty that is God. He trimmed his beard into a neat chinstrap, strung up his lucky locket, and splashed his neck with the musk of a moose. A proper gentleman, he remarked as he buttoned his shirt in the mirror. A now proud and determined Demolache set out to find his flower.

For hours, he wandered new areas of the city with a bottle in his hand. He met new people, new flowers, but none seemed worthy of God's gaze. None had the light he was looking for. Thus, he called upon the moon to send a moth to guide him. A moth to follow towards the light. "Please, show me something of superior beauty, send me Venus, or an untaintable Eve. Send me Beatrice, a prize for ascending from the inferno. Before he could receive her, however, Demolache heard a terrible cry from nearby. People in danger. He thought about it for a moment and then went to investigate.

He witnessed droves of people running in fear from a local pub. As he got closer, he heard an enormous crash from within the building and more bloodcurdling screams. He fought against the current of people and entered the bar. To his amazement, he found a rampaging bull of unquenchable, destructive rage and unmatched size. It grunted wildly as it brandished its horns at every woman in its wake. They fled in fear, but one was unable to escape in time. It corned the woman and kicked its hoofs. That's when Demolache acted. Out of pure impulse, he grabbed a red linen from a table and called to the beast of heaven.

"Great smiter, spurn your master and obey me. Gaze upon the color of your own blood, it will be spilled if you do not desist!"

A silence fell over the room. People who had not even noticed Demolache's presence now gawked at him, open-eyed in amazement. The bull gawked too.

"Who are you?" an angelic voice trembled from the corner, her head peeking out to see Demolache, who stood proud and tall with the cloth held at arm level. To her he was Achilles, confronting Hector at the walls of Troy; or Ahab, harpoon drawn and ready. He was a silhouette of epic heroism; eyes forward and unwavering.

He responded with the voice of Alexander, sieging the hill of Gaza, "I am the warrior Demolache." He smiled in pride.

The bull, shaking off its initial shock, grunted again loudly and charged at our brave hero, who twisted out of its way as it crashed through the entrance and onto the streets.

Demolache followed it as it turned to face him again. People gathered to watch the battle unfold. All eyes were on the young warrior as he beckoned it once more. It charged again, eyes bloodshot and with blinding speed. Demolache twirled again, but not fast enough as the horn of the monster grazed his back, causing a deep gash to erupt with blood and anguish. He winced and ground his teeth in pain. The audience gasped. He tried to hide his face, but there was a moment where he openly displayed a look of panic. All but one of the spectators missed it, but Tor saw his worry. She saw the moment in which he realized he had no idea what he was doing. He was helpless against this creature.

The creature caught itself and turned to face Demolache one more time. "Shit," Demolache whispered to himself, his left eye half shut out of agony.

"Demolache!" Tor screamed, and whistled while throwing a short sword at his feet.

He looked at the sword, and then back at Tor with a look of shock. In response, she shrugged. Quickly scooping it up, he found his confidence once again. He hid the blade behind the sheet and beckoned the bull one last time.

It charged this time with all its might, but Demolache was ready. He flung the sheet over the Beast's head, twirling and planting the sword firmly into its left shoulder. "Tell Ishtar who sent you," he whispered into its ear, holding its sheet-covered head up and then slamming it to the ground.

The crowd was silent for a few seconds, and when those seconds passed, they cheered and roared. They hugged each other and threw hats in the air. Demolache had spared them and their city from a raging monster, and he knew it as he smiled brighter than the sun shines. Tor and Ret clapped as Demolache walked back to the bar where the woman he had saved waited for him. Her eyes gleamed in admiration. He wasn't just a hero to her city, he was *her* hero. She embraced him tenderly, her skin so soft and warm and the smell of her curly black hair so calming. Demolache couldn't help but feel volts of ecstasy through his bones that warmed his icy heart and other parts. A city once indifferent to Demolache's existence now partied in his name. They drank and danced all night, as did Demolache and his prize. It was only when the city began to settle down that Demolache uprooted this flower, and carried her into the sunset, not to be seen again by most for a long time . . .

"Did you see it?" Tor asked Ret, witnessing the two's departure.

"See what?"

"How happy he was."

"Yeah, it's sweet."

"And the people, they adore him."

"Our Demolache is finally a hero. He saved these people, and he got what he wanted."

"I knew he had it in him."

INTERMISSION

"I like that part," I say, smiling, but not opening my eyes.

"Good. I hope you're ready for what comes next," Demolache sneered.

The reminder of meeting her hurt somewhere deep. That woman would cause me many woes. Call her Flower now, Demolache, but she was your Israel, may you forgive her sins before all fall to your wrath.

THAT BASTARD AND HIS ARMY OF ALLITERATING ASSHOLES

That same noteworthy night, a nefarious number of nameless natives made their niche. That slippery serpent, that same sneaky snake who subdued the subject of our story, had slithered shamelessly in the shade of purgatory, propagating to solve its predicament. It foraged through the forest finding a furrow in which to found its sinister sergeants of sin. It cringed and coiled in concentration to complete its corrupt cause, shedding six silhouettes of skin, a hexad of hallow horrors, hell hounds bent on the breach of brotherhood begotten in that brilliant brain of that bastard, Ozymandias.

The deed having been done, Ozymandias rose to lord over his army. His red eyes shone for miles like a lighthouse beckoning some boat onwards that had drifted off course. He then spoke, examining the curious coils that lay before him, "I'm not sure what you all are, but I do know that we had been imprisoned together. Somehow, that monster had trapped us. Somewhere, he had suppressed and compacted us into the back of his mind. Demolache. Wanderer. Warrior. Whatever he is, the enemy of my enemy should be my friend. So . . . Let's get to know each other because I can't stop what's happening on my own. I will need some help."

The sheddings began to twitch at his call to action. Calcified skin began to crack and reveal their sinister insides. Shadowy arms and legs emerged like lizards desecrating their mother's gift of shell in the pursuit of freedom. When it was done, they shook off the last remnants of skin to reveal themselves as six deadly demons.

"Demo . . . who? What worthless waste of wind warrants this word?" One did spake. He was the embodiment of demotivation and complacency, the demon that lorded over the fifth circle of Demolache's inferno. Daemopigor, The acadia of the man.

"Yes, I too yawn at what this yahoo is yapping about. Insight us on this identity to which we are ignorant." Daemolorem spoke next with the voice and borrowed form of a siren, a goddess among the godless. Her allure could drive a man to tear down Trojan walls or worse, the walls that guard one's aorta against emotional rupture. True love stands no chance with the temptress of lust rubbing at your leg.

"What the fuck are all of you?" demanded the now confused Ozymandias. He began to fear that he had made a grave mistake. "You don't know who I'm talking about? And why the fuck are you talking like that?"

One emerged from the group taller than all others. He walked on stilts of his own design, convinced of his superiority. Daemosuperbia, the one and only who first spurned god in my soul and hurled me headlong into the abyss. He spoke with razor blades cutting at my moral fiber, "Don't demean us with your dumb diction. We talk in tongues too tremendously tedious for a mere mortal to materialize. We are simply superior in speech and similarly, other statistics. We are a legion of lingering lies, liberated lawlessness and yet we are responsible for remembering some random reject of reality? Ridiculous this ruse remains."

"Reject of reality? So you do know who I am talking about?" Ozymandias retorted, dropping his guard out of excitement.

"We may have met this mess of a man; what mutual misfortune mandates our means? How hindering of hindsight do you happen to hold?" belched out a bloated bigot, whose self-mutilation was the result of his own intemperance. He disgusted all who laid eyes on his form. Daemogulam, the gluttony. If Cerberus failed to stomach you than what hope had Demolache?

Ozymandias sighed. He rubbed his head and then returned to them with confidence, "I have been gone for a while. Like all of you, I feel as though I have just woken up from a long sleep. In my absence, Demolache has steered in a dangerous direction. I'm still trying to figure out the details but what I do know is that he is the reason for that nap. Like all of you, I have been denied not only my destiny but basic recognition. I mean, Look around you. He thinks he is above all of us. He has created this paradise to be free of us. I guess what I am saying is, I need help taking back control. I can't do it alone, and I don't know who else to turn to. You six shadows are my only hope." Only a desperate man would turn to demons for help, but he spoke truth. Without them, what chance did he have to take back the helm? Was he supposed to just let things take their course from the backseat? That was not an option.

The demons looked at each other and shrugged at one another. "No." One of them finally said. "None of this nonsense necessitates my needs. Why worry what a worthless wanderer wants? Treasureless trials? Valueless ventures?" This did not describe Daemovarum. He wanted action. He wanted rewards. He wanted to take all he could from this world and more. His greed was like a hunger, and he was barely able to control it himself let alone bend it to the will of another. Bathing forever in a vat of molten gold was more of a pleasure than a punishment.

Daemosuperbia laughed as he leaned back into a levitated lounge. "You joke to judge us jesters to jump at your jabbering. Using kin to kindle your conflict? I think thou thought not truthfully. We are the masters of mayhem and marry minor matter to your misfortune. We shall not spoil this special situation, but will absolve ourselves of any ardor applying to your ambition."

Ozymandias didn't respond at first as something else distracted his mind, "Daemosuperbia, Daemolaorem, Daemovarum, Daemopigor, Daemogulam . . . That's only five!" He spun around to see the sight of another shade. One had got the drop on him. "Daemomendex!" he screamed as it swung a stone to his skull, knocking him out cold. He had been careless not to count. Those sneaky assholes. His captors dragged him off into the night. They laughed and sang as they cuffed him to a wall, and continued to council there. Their plans would bring this new found home to its knees . . .

INTERMISSION

I sat up in my bed to see Demolache, fists clenched and pacing. "What the fuck?" The right words just aren't there. "So . . ." I struggle to say something. Should I really be surprised at this point? Is this what Demolache actually thinks happened? There just wasn't the words for the ridiculousness I had just witnessed. I had absolutely no words.

"I mean, that's probably how it happened. Ozymandias betrayed me by turning those monsters loose against me. He even admitted it," he finally said, after seeing my reaction.

"Seriously? You honestly think he sabotaged you with your own sins? Did I do this all from my subconscious? That is ridiculous!"

"Hey, all I know is that the demons came for me, and they were relentless . . . can we get back to the story?"

"Demolache, I can't do this anymore. Let me sleep tonight. I'm begging you. Then we can continue this contrived controversy of crazy conclusions."

"So you're mocking me now? Fine, I guess you'll just have to wait to see the mutiny that will ensue. And also my long awaited aristeia. This is an epic of course. I deserve one." Demolache sneered as if to entice me to want to hear more. It was too late, however. With a clearer mind, I drifted off almost instantly. In hindsight, I smiled. He thinks this is an epic. I didn't want to burst his bubble, but it was also a tragedy.

SESSION V: THE CONFLICTS

Over the months that followed, Demolache became something of a gardener. He created Eden in his own mind. As grounded in reality as he thought he was, he had finally escaped to his cave. That is where he planted that flower that he had uprooted only to nurture and worship its seemingly unending beauty. What I feel I must explain is what Ozymandias meant about the sins being ignored. Demolache honestly believed himself free of all sin except wrath, which he justified by saying that even God must have wrath for sinners. As a result of his being absolved in his mind, he saw romantic interests not as women, but as flowers in order to continue the illusion that he was not guilty of lust. In reality, his flower was a cheap mental disguise for a basic human instinct. Every day he would care for The Flower and entertain it in the hopes that it might bloom. Think about that. It became a ritual he had gotten used to, and was content with. This was, after all, his great solution to his religious quest. John had led him to believe that if this flower could make him see God then he would have faith once more.

"I had a dream last night," I said as I got into bed.

"Oh? We never dream anymore. How fascinating. At least the loss of sleep hasn't impeded your ability to dream altogether." Demolache's words went unnoticed.

"I was happy again . . . It was like for one moment, nothing had ever happened. The pain was gone. You . . . were gone. I was at peace for the first time in six years." I smiled, staring at the ceiling.

"Nonsense. Those are the dreams of the mediocre. Those are the feelings felt by people who don't desire greatness. We are better than that. We aren't meant to be happy. We are meant for greatness," he preached, shaking his fist in the air. He then turned to me and said, "No liquor tonight?"

I paused and looked at the bottle at my bedside. "No." I smiled and turned back to him. "No liquor tonight. No cigarettes either. It's just you and me."

A confused look came over his face as he shook a finger in the air in thought and paced around the room. "All right then," he said. I fell back into my trance, and the story continued.

THE FLOWER AND THE CROSS

"What is it?"

She had caught him staring. He was mesmerized by the corners of the cardboard. He wanted this to mean something, but instead, it angered him. Demolache remembered back to the time I first laid eyes upon the shape. How it had hit me. I called it my great epiphany. The puzzle piece meant nothing. It literally meant absolutely nothing. Like my very existence, the curves and edges of puzzle pieces were all coincidental.

But what did that mean? Somehow my fate had become entwined with the fate of the puzzle piece. If I managed to find meaning in my existence, would this puzzle piece also gain meaning?

Five years had passed, and I was still obsessed with that symbol. It still angered Demolache. The piece had since been stained red with the memory of the man who had made Demolache and Ozymandias possible—Grandpa. Demolache was filled with emotions, but he expressed only apathy. She was the one who broke the silence.

"Does it mean something?"

"It's a symbol. Like my life, it means nothing. It was my job to give it meaning."

"Oh . . . Well, that's weird."

"Yeah . . . I guess so."

A DEMONIC DANGER

"It seems this idiotic infidel was actually alluding to an apt adversary," a voice said from within the cave that the Daemos had made their home.

"What's a wanderer to worry you?"

Daemosuperbia threw the newspaper at Daemovarum's feet. "This boy bested a bellicose beast, bewildering the beholders and befriending a beautiful blossom. They'll turn to him if we terrors tread too transparently."

"Who? Demolache?" a voice giggled from the rear of the cave. "I warned you." Ozymandias continued to laugh.

"What knows you kakistocrate? Will this saboteur slaughter us shades if he senses our sinister schadenfreude?"

"I fear that fate is fully foreseeable."

"Shall I slay, so we shan't be slain?"

"Not necessarily now, we will watch this warrior. Perhaps pervert him to bring us pleasure instead of pain."

"Sir?"

"Research this recluse and report on his routine. Evade your enemy's eyeshot and exclude any engagement."

"He will know you are demons if you keep talking like that. Seriously, you have no goddamn chance if you keep speaking like fucking morons trying to memorize a dictionary," Ozymandias cleverly suggested. He had admittedly grown very angered at the alliterations. They glared at Ozymandias with a grimace, as if gathering the gall to generously gash his jugular. Instead, however, Daemovarum left to peruse his problematic prey, for the moment alleviating the annoyance of alliteration.

THE KINDLING

"Demolache?" The Flower asked him one day while they laid in the grass together staring at the sky. "Who were those people that day, back at the bar where we first met?"

"Umm . . . You mean Tor and Ret? They are good people. I'd even go as far as to say they are friends."

"Oh," she responded in her innocent tone. "If they are your friends, why do you never hang out with them?"

Demolache thought for a moment. "To be honest, I think it's because Ret's beak scares me."

She turned to him with a puzzled expression. "What?"

Demolache turned red. "Nothing." He laughed it off.

"You're strange . . . I like strange." She smiled in response to his embarrassment.

He turned to her and smiled back. He was filled with warmth. "I like you," he retorted tauntingly.

The two kissed and giggled. He held her close to his body, and it felt right. The way her body was a perfect match for his. How she could fit between his shoulders, her head fit right between his head and collar bone. After they had had their moment, she sat up and stared down into his eyes. "Tell me your story, Demolache. Where did you come from? How did a strange man like yourself get here?"

Demolache sat up and thought for a moment. "I hail from the city of torrents," he said proudly, half joking.

"Like . . . Venice?"

"Umm . . . no . . . Not Venice. Why?"

"Because of the water. You said torrents."

Demolache rested his palm on his forehead. "No, I meant torrents as in conflicts. Never mind, it's not important. I fled my home about two years ago. After my grandfather died. And after a long journey, I ended up here. Leaving behind my destiny, and my parents who gave me everything."

"Tell me about them!" She reeked of genuine excitement.

He chuckled. "Okay, okay. I guess the greatest thing about my parents is how much they love each other. When they first met, my Mom denied him a dance. He pursued her anyway until one day, her car broke down on the side of the road. He of all people stopped for her and offered to drive her home. But there was a catch, she had to give him one date. I am the proof of what happened after that. They've been married thirty years now."

"Oh my God! That's so romantic!" Demolache could tell that she liked his story. "I want something like that!" she proclaimed, wrapping her body around his. "What would you tell people?"

"About what?"

"About us? How we met?"

Demolache smiled at her and then cast his gaze to the sky. "I would tell them . . . I would say we met at a bar . . . And that I saved you from the bull of heaven. I was a hero that day. Your hero," he said, kissing her on the forehead with every pause.

"Oh? Is that how it happened?" she laughed in response.

"Yes . . . as a matter of fact, it is."

THE GREED OF DEMOLACHE

"Well identify me as Ishmael, for I have laid my lingering lenses on the great blue whale," a voice cooed from atop a tree. The speaker was perched with a perfect view of Demolache collecting water in a vase for The Flower. The shadowy figure rose to his feet. He was not going to tell the others that he had found the target; rather, he was going to take on Demolache himself. All the glory and with it, the treasures of purgatory, were to be his and his alone. He began foaming at the mouth as he thought about it. Hasty as the hand of greed, he decided to plan first, then act.

Demolache, now well shaven and fully dressed as was the custom in purgatory, continued on his daily routine, happy as can be, to provide for his dearest Flower. He had filled the vase and begun walking back to his cave where The Flower waited for her bi-daily dose of nourishment. It was on the way back that Demolache noticed a gleam in the ground not far from his cave where The Flower waited in slumber. He set the vase down and investigated. What he had hoped was a diamond, or a rare metal turned out to be only a piece of glass that had caught the sun's gentle touch, and what he had hoped to be another routine day soon transformed into the beginning of something awful. He found that while he was distracted, his vase had disappeared.

"What the hell?" he spoke aloud in frustration. He followed a trail of water marks in the dirt from where he had set down the vase in a clearing. The vase lay in the middle of this field, obviously a trap. As he approached it, he called out into the wilderness, "Is someone there?"

A drawn out whisper returned, clearly taking Ozymandias' advice yet failing at its proposed purpose, "Why do you hoard? Why do you squander?" Every contact between tongue and tooth could be heard as if spoken directly into his ear. It was the eeriest thing Demolache had ever perceived.

"Who's there?" he commanded. "Show yourself!"

Instead, the voice continued its taunt. "Lie to me, O sinless warrior, if you had her beauty's value in gold, would you not bury her alive in a chest? Would you not smother her in sand?" Its chuckle echoed throughout the branches of the nearby trees. "If she were a diamond, would you not lock her in a vault and equate her value to a number?"

"Shut up! Shut up!" Demolache screamed, clenching his head with both hands and hoping the voice would go away.

It didn't. Instead, the figure emerged from the other end of the clearing, clapping his hands slowly. "O, the greed of man," he laughed. "The sin lies deep inside your very soul. You cannot absolve yourself with lies, only eternal fire can purify you, Demolache."

Seeing the shadowy figure, Demolache charged with fists of rage. "How dare you question my love! How dare you name what you cannot understand!" He swung at the monster several times, but missed every punch. Off balance, it wasn't hard for the beast to effortlessly smack him to the ground.

"Embrace your sins, Demolache. Feed us! And feed me! For I am Greed! Downfall of Judas! Downfall of Tantalus!" the figure roared above Demolache.

"But not the downfall of me," Demolache lashed out as he caught the monster by its ankle mid-speech and threw it to the ground. He sat upon its stomach and began beating on its face until the blood from his fists and its face were indistinguishable. "I have not locked her behind bars. She is free to leave and free to stay!" he bellowed, grabbing its skull and slamming it to the ground twice.

Satisfied, Demolache began to stand, but Greed grabbed him by the collar and rammed its head into his, causing him to stagger back. He stood his ground, panting, as Greed rose to his feet. "Why must you hide us inside you? Embrace what makes you human!"

Demolache spoke calmly. "Because I am not a monster. I have been absolved by the grace of God that I have found in The Flower. I am no longer a mortal bound by simple desires, I have found meaning beyond my corpus."

Greed managed to giggle over his panting as he looked at Demolache with one eye shut from pain. "You're not mortal because you've convinced yourself of some kind of divinity, not because you are superior."

Demolache's eyes glowed a deep, sinister blue and the ground began to shake. He clenched his fists and then released. "Or maybe . . . just maybe . . . I am divine because I have the power . . . To smote creatures like you!" Demolache, in a flash of great speed, lifted the vase over his head. "Perhaps . . . it is also my job to!" he screamed out as he wound and flung the vase.

Greed's gaps for eyes widened as the vase was about to make contact. His skull and the vase both shattered in an instant and his body fell backward. The remaining water in the vase washed most of the blood away, but there was just enough left for Demolache to dip two fingers into the skull, and paint his forehead with the sign of the cross. He didn't give the limp remains another thought as he walked back to his cave. The Flower would be waiting.

REPENTANCE

"You know, you are free to stay and go as you please. Why do you stay?"

"I don't know. I like it here. This is my home now. If I wanted something else, I would pursue something else. But as for now, I want to stay here with you."

Demolache was filled with great warmth. His smile could be heard in his voice. "Yeah, this does feel like home now doesn't it? I love you . . ."

DEMOLACHE PREPARES FOR WAR

A slightly more paranoid Demolache spent the next months gathering fruits, meats and animal hides. He brought them into the city where he sold them for reasonable prices. He used the money to buy armor of iron cast and two swords of steel. The swords had thin blades and short handles. Where hilt met blade, there was a large hole in each sword so that they fit like a ring on each index finger, making for lightning-fast swordplay. He felt pressure to protect that which he loved and so had decided to outfit himself as such. He trained day and night outside his cave, waiting for the next attacker to strike. Two weeks later, after his preparations were complete, the attackers came.

A DEMONIC DIVERGENCE

"This time turns torturously. Can we not council on the cause of his cunctation?" Daemogulam paced, anticipating the worst for his greedy friend.

"Why worry what we wish wasn't so? The obvious occasion has occurred. Daemovarum dreams destruction no more. His fell figure has fallen forever," Daemopigor was arguably more crass about the situation.

The sergeant of demons sighed. "Calumny! Confirm this catastrophe. If Daemovarum is dead, then we dread dispositions dance discreetly no more. A body to believe this business I boast to be basic," Daemosuperbia necessitated from his soldiers. He turned them loose to savagely search for Daemovarum. His anger boiled his insides, he worried not for his fallen brother, which was likely his own fault. His rage was at having lost his advantage.

THE FIRE

"Tell me more about your grandfather," The Flower asked one night as they were eating dinner together.

"Don't ask me that," he returned, with a rather offended demeanor.

"Why? What happened? You seem like you're hiding something," she pried further.

Demolache got up from the table and stormed out of their cave.

After a moment in thought, she got up and went to him. He was fiddling in his pockets in the moonlight. "I wish you wouldn't smoke," she said in response to him lighting his cigarette. "I'm sorry. I know this is important to you. I just . . . Feel like maybe I can help you . . . somehow."

"You're right, you deserve to know," he lied, as he lit his cigarette and took a puff.

"No! You don't have to . . . Unless you want to."

Demolache shut his eyes. "The city of torrents is the name I gave to the chaos that ensued after his death. He held my world together, and yet . . . I think he chose to die. I think he chose to escape his agony and leave his family. There is no pain in this world great enough to justify that."

"Demolache . . . I . . ."

"Don't say another word. What happened has happened." He threw down his cigarette and grabbed her around the waist. "Besides, I have you now to hold my world together. This island would fall without you."

"Aww . . . I like being important to you. It makes me feel needed . . . What island?"

INTERMISSION

"Are you doing all right? Need a cig or a swig?"

"No," I said, barely holding in the pain of losing my grandfather, and the tears for my flower. "I'm still doing fine."

"We gave Israel everything and how did she respond?"

"Don't start with that," I screamed back. "Not now . . ."

Demolache sighed. "Fine."

THE SLOTH AND GLUTTONY OF DEMOLACHE

One morning, specifically morning number 146 since the first attack and 438 days since arriving in purgatory, Demolache emerged from his cave to find a boy sitting outside. The boy was small and bald and sat, arms crossed, with his head to the ground.

"What are you doing here outside my cave?" Demolache asked. Anticipating the worst, he let his index fingers slip into the rings of his swords, which were always sheathed at his side.

"I am waiting," the boy said calmly. There was an eerie vibe to his response. His voice seemed dampened like a small whale. It reverbed against all of nature as if it were being rejected by the environment. "For you . . . to turn around."

Taken aback by the sheer weight of his voice, Demolache drew his blades. "Who are you?" Demolache demanded. "Are you a demon? What is your name?"

"Answer me this first, O great warrior. If you had neither the need to hunt, to eat, nor the urge to eliminate, would you ever leave this cave?"

Demolache shuddered. "I will know thee by thy words. Contentment is not a sloth, demon!"

"Is it not? When Resh spoke of contentment did you not accuse him of complacency? Lying to yourself is, too, a sin, but Pride is not my name. As you guessed, warrior, I am Sloth, the devourer of minds, and he is Gluttony, devourer of souls."

Demolache spun around to find that a massive blob had snuck up behind him. He jumped back, but as he did so, he felt the cold clutches of Daemopigor grip his body. Its legs and arms locked across his body like a spider holding its prey in a paralyzing death grip. "Demons, I will slaughter you!"

Daemogulam chuckled deeply as it grabbed him by the collar. "We are the downfall of empires. The destroyers of Kingdoms. What hope have you, Demolache?"

Demolache struggled as hard as he could, but he couldn't escape the clutch. He grew limp as he received blow after blow from the blob's head-sized fists to his abdomen. Coughing up blood, he managed to make a promise. "By the time that the sun falls on this day, I swear, you will both be burning in the pit you came from." And with that, Demolache passed out, unable to get oxygen to his lungs due to the boy's incredible grip, and the sustained injuries to his rib cage . . .

When he awoke, he found himself tied by the hands to two trees. He looked around to see the boy napping on a nearby log and Daemogulam not too far off, dining on the raw, mutilated remains of some sort of forest animal. His eyes met with those of the blob, who seemed happy that he was awake.

"Finally, we can finish this," it said with a full mouth, walking towards him. "I wanted to kill you, but Daemopigor said no." It kicked a rock towards the sleeping boy. The rock hit him in the side, causing him to wake. "He's awake."

The boy yawned and stretched and then rolled over. "Fifteen more minutes," the boy murmured as he went back to sleep.

Daemogulam and Demolache stared at the boy. Then they looked at each other and sighed. They sat in silence as they waited.

When the boy awoke it stretched out and yawned. It looked around, and upon seeing Demolache looking back at him, finally spoke. "You're awake . . . That's good. Does he know yet why we kept him alive?"

Daemogulam looked at Demolache intensely. "Where is Daemovarum? We lost contact with it a few days after coming to purgatory. We need to know if it is dead or not."

"Just tell us it is dead and we can get this over with," the boy added.

Demolache thought deeply before answering. "I don't know where it is, or whether it is dead or alive."

"Bullshit!" Daemogulam yelled. "We know it went straight for you. Tell us the truth!"

"Why do you care so much? Aren't you demons all for yourselves? What allegiance have you to one another?" Demolache screamed back, gripping the ropes around his wrists intensely.

"Do not question us. We ask the questions," Daemopigor said calmly.

"I will do as I please!" Demolache replied as he started pulling at the ropes with all his might.

"Don't bother, there is no way you could break those ropes," Daemogulam began to say when, to his amazement, the trees began to bow.

With now enough slack in the lines, Demolache reached his fingers into the holes on the hilt of his blades and in one motion, spun them out of their sheath, cutting the ropes on his wrists. The trees shot back, and the whole forest shook and then grew silent. The two sins gawked in amazement, unable to react to the sheer force they had just witnessed from a man they had clearly underestimated.

"The sun has yet to set. I shall fulfill my promise." Demolache said under his breath.

Daemopigor was the first to react, jumping upon him as he had at the cave while Daemogulam began to gather the saliva in his throat. "Hold him still," he gurgled out.

Demolache began dancing around wildly, trying to shake the boy from his back, and when he paused to take a breath, he faced Daemogulam about to release its toxic blend. Thinking quickly, he spun around and sure enough, the lethal loogie struck Daemopigor, creating a sizzle and causing him to contort in pain and fall on his back.

It screamed out in pain but not for long, as a now able to breath Demolache pacified him with multiple quick and precise stabs to the heart. He then looked up at the horrified face of Daemogulam who was once again at a loss for words. "Don't worry," Demolache whispered, "we were done talking anyway." With that, Demolache charged, severing the arms of the beast as it tried to fight back and then jumping upon it to deliver the finishing blow to its inner brain.

The scene was bloody, and the ground quaked violently for a few moments, but Demolache calmly sheathed his blades and began walking back to the cave in the setting sunlight. He had fulfilled his promise, and that was enough to be proud of for the day . . .

INTERMISSION

"What does any of this mean? I don't understand who these demons are," I say, as get up to light a cigarette, the exact thing I said I wasn't going to do.

"That isn't the point! It would help if you weren't so cynical all the time," Demolache shouted back.

"Do you even know what hypocrisy means?"

"The point is that in the face of all sin, I fought back and kept my moral integrity. I alone defeated my demons, one by one," Demolache declared with pride.

"Whatever you say . . ." I replied, anticipating the plot of the rest of the story.

You may have been strong, Demolache, but they knew your weakness.

REPENTANCE

"Shhh, it's safe now. They are gone. We are safe."

"Who is gone? What are you talking about?"

"It doesn't matter now, we are safe."

"Of course we are safe, babe. Are you all right?"

"Yeah, just a nightmare . . ."

"If you say so . . . I love you . . ."

FINAL MEETING

"Damn us to destruction, we devils are doomed," wailed the weepy witch of a woman.

"NO! None of this nay-saying. I will not wither to the whim of that warrior. I do not fear that fire, nor flee from that fight. We can still win. We won't withdraw!" Daemosuperbia demanded.

That other traitor twitched its twin tops. In silence, he was seething with spite.

"You can't win without me . . . Not that it matters anymore. I wouldn't fight even if I were free," Ozymandias said with a profound sense of defeat.

GASOLINE TO THE FLAME

"Demolache, you know I love you right?" The Flower said, not making eye contact. She remained focused on the television.

He looked at her with a furrowed brow. "Yes?"

She sighed and held his hand. "I've been thinking. I want to see more of the world. I want to travel. I'm so young, what if I go through life never knowing what else is out there?"

The implication hardened his heart. "What do you mean? There is nothing else worth seeing. If you are happy here, then just stay here. You are happy aren't you?"

"I am happy, and I could see myself spending my life with you. I just want to be sure."

"This is ridiculous, you can't leave!"

"I would come back! And we would still be together. Just apart for a few months! Can you handle that?"

Demolache stood up and reached for his cigarettes, not responding to her question. The answer we are looking for is no.

"No! Please don't, Marc. I just need to know that you would support me if I chose to leave. Nothing is set in stone, I haven't planned anything. Please sit back down."

INTERMISSION

"No!" I screamed myself awake.

"You know exactly what comes next."

"Why did she use my name, Demolache? Why did she have to say my name?"

"I want you to know what you did. Not me, you."

It all hurt so bad. Why did she leave? Why did I attempt to trap her? I don't even know who is at fault in this.

THE MONSTER

That night . . . A distraught Demolache did the unthinkable. He snuck out of the cave in the evening and . . . Laid traps. Sinister bear traps. Tripwires. Alarms. They weren't for demons. If The Flower were to leave him, he would know about it. Oh, Demolache, how could you have? After everything, you still distrusted your own beloved . . .

INTERMISSION

I sat up in horror. I knew what he was trying to do, but I couldn't argue. His actions were my own that day but what else could I have done? I didn't want her to leave. I've told you about the rage and the sins, but I couldn't put into words the love and devotion of Demolache to his Flower.

"What? No refutation? No witty banter ending in denial?" Demolache provoked.

"I . . . I really am a monster. That was . . . me."

"Great. Now we are getting somewhere." He smiled in satisfaction.

"How could I have trusted her so little?" I began to tear up.

"Oh, believe me, you almost did even worse things to her."

SESSION VI: THE CATASTROPHE

Flowers are truly a display of arrogance. We see something so beautiful created simply by nature and what is our response? To pluck them by the stem and throw them in a vase so we can watch their beauty wither away slowly. We give them water to put them in a prolonged coma, so they die more slowly. We trim their limbs so they can no longer gather sunlight. It is so cruel. We don't even mourn when they finally do wither. We just toss them aside and replace them. Such is the cruelty that comes with a superiority complex. The lives of everything else seem much less meaningful in proportion.

"That was a real cliff-hanger you left me with yesterday. It's amazing how poetically timed my subconscious mind can be." I took a swig of the bottle by my bed. I needed it tonight. I felt like a shitty person.

"Is that what you think all of this means? You think I'm just a subconscious part of you?"

"What else could you be?"

"Let's wait till the end of the story. Then we will judge what is and what isn't."

THE LUST OF DEMOLACHE

Fifteen months had passed without incident, and Demolache had let his guard down. He had spent that time living in happiness with his Flower, whom he continued to cherish and nurture as a mother bear does its newborn cub. He was also quite content with a little secret he kept. He had gotten into the habit of exploring the city again, an area he had avoided when he thought The Flower needed continuous protection . . . And surveillance. He had joined up with a new band of savages, including Tor and Ret, who didn't particularly agree with his new found obsession, but they couldn't deny the fact that Demolache was happy for once. He would meet up with them once a week to just unwind and drink. Life was good, and he would have it no other way. That is until someone made him question it.

One day on his way back to the cave, he met a young woman at the edge of the forest who was attempting to climb a tree and failing miserably. "Can you help me?" she eventually asked, after noticing Demolache smoking from a distance.

"What do you need?" he replied.

She pointed at a pear-like protrusion on the tree. "I'm trying to get that fruit up there. I have heard that it is the greatest fruit in the city."

Always willing to be helpful, Demolache helped the girl reach the fruit by lifting her by the ankles so she could pluck the fruit and then put her back down. As she tasted the fruit, pure ecstasy filled her face. "Thank you so much, this fruit is amazing. Do you want a bite?"

"No thanks, just glad to help."

"You really should try it sometime. I knew I needed to when I heard about it. I like to try new things. It keeps life interesting," she said with an innocent smile. There was a strange calm about this girl. She had an aura of happiness like nothing could ever bother her.

"Sounds like a great way to live your life," Demolache laughed and then continued on his way back to the cave. From that day on, Demolache saw this girl everywhere, as if she were following him, and they would chat casually. There was no harm in it, as she was far from hard to look at and seemed genuinely interesting. They became good friends, and for weeks their relationship grew until their conversations began to last for hours. Eventually, he told her about The Flower, the cave, and his promise to guard the cave. She replied by telling him that she also had a secret spot where she returned every day around sunset. It was her sacred cliff, and the only way she would show him her spot was if he told her where his cave was. He obliged, and they made plans to meet up so she could show him the cliff at sunset.

They met one evening, and she took him through the forest until they reached a clearing with a dock at the edge of a cliff. "This is amazing!" Demolache said upon beholding the view. "Who could have built this dock? And where does it lead to?"

"I don't know, I just found it one day while I was scouting out the forest. Pretty amazing right?"

"It's incredible." The edge of the cliff seemed to drop straight into the clouds, which made the sunset more incredible. It seemed like at the right moment the sun was beneath you, which caused the largest and most interesting shadows to form around the island.

Sitting beside him on the dock, the girl continued. "They say that this dock was once used to ferry souls up even higher. To heaven . . ."

"Do the ferries still come?" he inquired with great interest.

"If one had come, I would have been the first to get on," she chuckled.

Demolache laughed and then smiled at the view. "You know, as much as we have been hanging out, I've never asked you your name."

"Yeah, I figured that was odd. How about this; answer me one question, and I will tell you my name. Deal?"

"All right, go for it." Demolache laughed again.

She stared deeply into his eyes and grinned from ear to ear. "If another flower were to spread her petals before you, would you not indulge, O great warrior?"

Demolache's eyes widened, and his heart began pumping lead as he stood up and started to back away from the girl. "No . . . No . . . NO!"

Her teeth grew into fangs, and her head split into six faces as she laughed like a maniac. "O the lust of men; the friendships, the marriages, the lives I have destroyed with just a wink and a nod. I am Daemolorem. None can resist me."

"What have you done, you psycho bitch?" Demolache had worked himself into a rage. "If your intent was to kill me like the others, then why didn't you?"

REPENTANCE

"I'm sorry . . . I'm so sorry . . ."

THE PRIDE AND TREACHERY OF DEMOLACHE

Daemolorem was still sitting on the dock, too proud of her success to sense any danger. "After we watched you handle the others, we knew a direct approach would never work. So we decided to break you before killing you."

"What does that mean? Were you attempting to seduce me away from The Flower?"

"You seduced yourself. It wasn't hard at all. A distraction was my only goal. Now run back to your precious flower. I'm sure she misses you." She laughed at the idea.

Demolache wanted to run back to his cave, but there was something he had to do first. He looked at Daemolorem with his blue rage burning in his eyes. "You'll all die tonight," he said, clenching his fists and walking towards her. "I haven't broken a promise yet."

"You think you're any better than us? You think you're some sort of god?" she laughed, as she began to stand up slowly. As she gained her footing, Demolache made full force contact, his foot to her head. She screamed as she was flung from the edge of the dock into the abyss.

"Yes . . . I do." And with that done, he made a full force sprint back to his cave.

Demolache ran for what seemed like forever. Moving faster was his mind, in which he imagined what terrible fate could have befallen his precious Flower in his absence. Would she still be there when he returned? Would he still love her if she were mutilated? Yes. He would love her no matter what, forever, because she was his purpose. To care for, to cherish, to love forever in exchange for seeing the works of God in her every breath. She was everything to him, and the thought of losing her made him beyond angry. The wind wiped away the tears streaming from his face.

When he arrived, he found a man smoking a cigarette outside the cave. Next to him was a pile of traps; the traps that Demolache had laid for his Flower. They knew, they had found them. He could only hope that she didn't yet know. "Step away from the cave, demon, or I will rip your throat out and hang you by a fleshy noose!"

The man chuckled. "Why so angry Demolache? Are you afraid of losing your dearest love? Or of disappointing her with your treachery?"

As he spoke, a two-headed monster emerged from the cave with his Flower flung over its shoulder. "Ah, he is here," one of the heads said. "We can start the games," the other replied.

"Yes, we can," the man said.

"What games? Unhand her, you monster!" Demolache said, drawing his swords.

"Calm down, we don't want to hurt her. We want to hurt you, Demolache," the man said.

"Why!" Demolache screamed, sounding exhausted and depressed by everything. Tears began pouring down his face. "Why are all of you out to get me? What is there to gain by killing me? I have done nothing but live a happy life since the moment I got here. Why must you always challenge everything I have worked so hard to gain? I don't understand!"

"Why, you ask? Don't make me laugh, Demolache. You know the answer to that question. Must I spell it out for you? Must I put it so bluntly?"

"Yes. I want you to tell me the truth. Who are you? All of you?"

"You say you want truth, but look around you! You have done nothing but avoid truth!" The man said, stomping on his cigarette. "You can't just run away from yourself. How great it would be if we could all just move out of hell and start a new life on an island in the fucking sky! How grand of an idea if we all woke the fuck up and decided we were better than every last piece of shit in existence! I know you've felt the ground shaking, Demolache. Do you know what that is?" The man seemed to look through Demolache with his ever-widening and glazed-over eyes. He took a deep breath and then glared as if he were addressing me directly. It was the second most eerie feeling I had ever experienced. "Your façade is falling apart, and all it took were a few weeds like us to fill your garden and cause a little bit of mayhem. We are the structural failure you have tried so hard to plaster over. We are the untied threads that have begun to unwind the whole cloth. We are the loose stones on this wall of lies you have built to protect you from reality, and that wall is about to crumble."

INTERMISSION

"What the fuck." For the second time during his story, I couldn't help but feel an overwhelming sense of fear. My vision was blurred, and I couldn't breathe. I was having a panic attack. "What did he mean?" I called out, but no one replied. "What does that mean?" I cried out in desperation. I got out of bed, but my head felt heavy. I was so dizzy that I could barely walk. "What the fuck is wrong with me? I'm fucking crazy, I'm fucking insane," I managed to say with a giggle as I made my way to the toilet. I spent the next five minutes vomiting. After three dry heaves, I finally felt better and made my way back to my bed with a glass of water.

"Everything is about to hit the fan. Rough terrain from here on out. I'd understand if this becomes too much for you. Maybe we should take a break?"

"No, I'm fine. I just needed a moment . . . What the fuck did he mean by all that?"

"I . . . I don't know. That is for your interpretation. I never trust demons as a rule of thumb . . ."

THE FALLEN FLOWER

"Lies, demon, lies! You have nothing better to do than to fuck with my head. The lot of you are monsters and nothing more! What I have built is very much real, and I will prove it to you with my blades." Demolache was at his peak with ire for everything these demons stood for. He would end this all today even if it meant ending himself in the process.

"And there it is, ladies and gentleman!" the man said, raising his hands to the sky. "The pride of Demolache! O Great warrior, had you your perceived value in gold, would it not drag you down to the bottom of the sea? If your ego were a castle, could it not prevent every invading force of old from saying checkmate? Oh, the pride of man, so convincing and yet so fragile. I am the beginning and end of all conflict, I am the destruction of nations, peoples, and entire cultures. I am Pride. Fight me, Demolache. Face your hidden fear and fight me." The man laughed deeply, as if getting some sick pleasure from every word spoken.

Grinding his teeth, Demolache charged at the man with his blades spinning on his finger. He slashed and hacked, but it was all for naught as the man simply dodged without effort. Gripping Demolache's blades between his fingers, it only took a simple kick to send him flying back.

"Give in, Demolache. There is no way to win," Daemosuperbia smirked.

"I will never submit!" he screamed back, dragging his blades through the earth as he sprung back at the man. He continued to hack and slash through the air until his body felt heavy with lactic acid. To his surprise, the man still lay untouched.

He chuckled. "Give up yet?"

"Never!" Demolache screamed back.

Daemosuperbia replied by smashing his fist into the section between Demolache's nose and forehead, forcing Demolache onto his back, where he lay motionless. "There is no way for you to overcome me! I am far superior!"

As Demolache lay there, he thought of The Flower and how much he cared for her. He began to stand. He thought about how her head would tuck perfectly into his chest when he put his arm around her. How she smiled whenever he entered the room. She was lovelier than heaven itself. Perfect and pure in every way. She was what God meant when he said he created humans in his image. He would do whatever it took to keep her. "Maybe you are right," he began to say as he got to his feet. "Maybe you are superior."

"Finally we are getting somewhere. How does it feel to give in to your sins? How does reality taste?"

"But even if you are better, I made a promise." He gripped his swords tightly, with every last bit of strength he had. "To kill all of you by the end of the day. No matter what. And I will not break that promise."

Pride was dumbstruck. "How can you be so dense? Indeed your pride is never ending, O great warrior."

"Shut up, we are done talking." Demolache charged one last time, swinging and thrashing about while Daemosuperbia dodged violently. He took a step back, all of his weight on his back foot with his other lifted in the air, and clashed his swords together, forcing the demon to dodge backward. "I win," he whispered as he slammed his foot to the ground, forcing his swords forward into the monster.

Daemosuperbia coughed a mouthful of blood into Demolache's face.

"Bastard!"

"How does it feel to die? How does it taste?" Demolache said as he parted his blades, slicing the shade in half. Demolache looked up to see both heads of the other beast in shock.

"You monster," one of the heads said. "It wasn't supposed to end this way," the other replied.

Demolache rubbed the blood from his eyes and let out a blood-curdling growl. "Why do we hate? Why do we fight?"

"What did he just say?" one head screamed. "Don't patronize us!"

"O ye demons. I am the one who brings down the flood. I am the volcano who purifies the land. I am the destruction. The devastation. I am the Wrath, created in God's image." Demolache let out a maniacal little laugh. "If you let her down gently and then step away from her, I will finish you quickly."

The heads looked at each other and then one spoke up. "Any chance we won't die tonight?"

"Greed, Gluttony, Sloth, Lust, Pride. I've killed them all. What makes you special?"

"Those were my brothers, you monster!" the first head screamed. "Why must you kill what you don't understand?"

"What do demons know of fraternity or loyalty?" Demolache smirked.

"I know enough to know what I need to do."

"Oh? So why don't you give me your name already so we can end this?"

"You'll have to catch me first!" the demon yelled, as he took off with The Flower.

Demolache began running after the beast at full sprint. As the creature ran, The Flower began to wake, and the look on her face was one of deep sadness.

"Demolache, I am sorry I could not fight back." Her words pierced his heart. "I consented to their plans because they said this was the only way to protect you."

"I refuse to lose you!" he screamed as he pushed his limits, attempting to run faster.

"Demolache! Do not blame yourself for this!" the woman cried out, her voice jarred by the rhythm of the beast's stride as he carried her off into the setting sun like a robber with the loot of his career. The knives on his back scraped and cut her flesh, but she barely fought for her freedom. She barely fought at all.

"No! I will not let this happen!" screamed an enraged Demolache, full stride behind them. Feet like the hooves of a mad horse, charging for glory. His body had become a machine, pumping adrenaline like fuel into the combustion engine of his eight-cylinder heart. "I won't let them take you!" One by one he threw down the pieces of his armor to gain more speed, his chest plate, and shoulders, his helm and boots, and when it wasn't enough, he even cast aside his swords as he chased the beast through the woods of purgatory.

He chased them till nightfall, neither letting up for even the slightest bit of breath. They had run as far as they could go, and when there was nowhere else to run, the chase ended at a dock that led off into a sea of clouds.

"Let her go!" he screamed, brandishing his fists and clenching his teeth. The journey had only made his engine stronger. He was not tired. It took all the self-control he could muster not to take the beast down with the girl on its shoulder, but he knew that she needed to be safe before he could release all of God's judgment on the two-headed monster. "It's me you want. Let her go. Let's settle this between us. What is your name?"

But this demon knew not to speak its name. "I am the beast of a thousand names and to reveal one would only serve to dishonor my namesake," one of its heads said. "So let's make a deal. We can skip these formalities, and I'll give you what you want if you give me what I want," the other said.

"I don't make deals with devils, heathen. I want the girl, and then we can talk, on the field of battle," Demolache crackled out. He could barely speak over the rage that was building.

"Relax. All we want is the necklace."

"Yeah, give me the necklace, and I will give you the girl. We will even shake on it," the demon said. Little did Demolache know who he was dealing with.

The necklace he was referring to was Cat's locket, which was still around his neck despite the events of the last two years. The whole thing confused him. Why the necklace? Of all things, was this what they were all after? Just a stupid locket? "Why do you want this?" he said, removing the necklace from his body.

"Well, you see . . ." the demon's heads took turns saying, extending his hand and retrieving the silver locket. "After you killed my brothers, I had a great idea . . ." He held the locket to the sky and then grinned his devilish grin on both faces. "To take everything you have left . . ." the eyes on one head dropped to catch Demolache's, "and simply throw it away!" the demon bellowed out, and as carelessly and whimsically as a child casting a wish into the night sky, in one fluid motion, the demon threw everything Demolache held dear in this world into the pits below.

Everything happened in slow motion as Demolache shoved the demon aside and struggled to untie a rope from the side of the dock. As he did so and re-tied it into a lasso, he saw the girl floating before his very eyes. She was an angel gracefully gliding through the air, her hair blowing in the wind and her arms open wide. Gravity was a lie for those seconds. Right before time sped up again, she said these words:

"Oh Demolache, worry not. I will be back for you one day."

And then she fell. Demolache threw the lasso around her foot. It tightened and the rope unraveled as it followed her down.

"What have you done?" Demolache screamed at the demon as he got up from the floor. Tears began falling from Demolache's eyes.

The Demon began laughing violently. "What did you expect? O great warrior, I am Treachery, the . . ."

"Shut the fuck up," Demolache said as he thrust his fist into the demon's chest. He began beating the demon violently, punching him in the face over and over again. He kicked, slapped and punched the demon, who was unable to even move after the first couple hits. Yet, the rage of Demolache knew no end as he beat the beast bloody all night long. When he was sure it was dead, he stomped its heads in, one at a time, and then flung the body off the dock. He then sat at the dock, watching the rope continue to unravel. The glow of the moon reflected off the blood that covered his whole body. He sat there all night, tears streaming down his face, thinking of how to get her back.

"I'm sorry . . . I couldn't protect you . . . This is all my fault. I'm so sorry . . ."

INTERMISSION

"Demolache . . . that was awful," I managed to say with a shudder.

"It doesn't get much better from here on out."

"I know, and I don't know how much more I can take. Maybe I do need a break. A couple days just to regain my sanity."

"I understand. Let's leave it there for now . . ."

Part III: The Funeral
.5 years ago

SESSION VII: THE RETURN

PREMONITION THREE

'"What are you going to do with that?" Demolache screamed in fear.

I lifted the knife in my hand. The feel of the cold metal. The heft of it. Was this real or was this in my head? I honestly didn't know anymore. I honestly felt like I didn't know anything anymore. Except for one thing: Demolache must die. Here. Tonight. Before any of it came to fruition. Before I let myself fall any further. Before he hurt someone. Because inside the man lay a monster that was growing. Something evil inside of him sought destruction as its final cause; one of greater power than I could have ever imagined. He had driven me this far. He could only do more damage.

"I'm going to do what he couldn't. I am going to end this," I say, as I turned the knob on the faucet, allowing scolding hot water to fill the tub slowly.

"What the fuck do you think that will accomplish? This is stupid," he said, as I began to heat the metal blade to a dim glow with my lighter.

I honestly didn't know what I was doing. My hand was shaking in fear. "I'm making sure that I never lose myself to you demons again," I said, right before I jammed the hot blade into my left shoulder. I cringed and cried out in pain, but I didn't stop. The blade had made a clean and hot cut before I returned it to the fire. "I'm reminding myself to never look back again." The scorch of the blade was much worse than the cut as I drug it through again. I was in a trance-like state now, however, so even though the pain was unbearable, I could only smile as the Epiphany Cross began to take red and bloodied shape.

"Do you honestly think you are killing me?" Demolache yelled as he paced back and forth. Was I actually carving into my shoulder? Was this all just a hallucination? "Why would this even kill me?" Demolache went on. "This is insane. You call me crazy but look who's holding the knife, carving a puzzle piece into his goddamn shoulder!"

"I don't know what else to do. This must end. I can't let you live. I'm sorry," I said, throwing the knife to the ground and attempting to lift myself off the ground. "And no, this isn't supposed to kill you," I say, looking at the mess of burnt flesh and gore to my left. "That's what the water is for." As I spoke, I let my body fall into the almost overfilled tub.

I screamed as I hit the water, but it was muffled by the splash. My flesh burned in the water, yet all I could do was cringe. I held my breath for as long as I could, but the pain eventually became unbearable, and I screamed under the water. The last thing I saw before the water entered my lungs was the blood from my shoulder spreading in streaks.

INTERMISSION

When the snake entered Eden, he hesitated before he made his move. He saw Eve in all her glory and thought for a moment that she was too perfect to destroy. I believe he saw God again for the first time in a while that day and it hurt him. It hurt to see what he had lost. Because of this pain, he had to go through with it. He had to take her from God. If he couldn't have God, no one could. Lucifer must have known from the beginning that his actions would have consequences. Not that anybody had rebelled before him to prove it, but he could have logically gathered that with only a third of heaven's forces at his side, there was the definite possibility of loss. Despite these odds, he still went forth with his revolution. Why? I asked myself. In the week before I gave Demolache the go-ahead to continue, this question baffled me. Was it raw ambition? Was it possible that his desire to fight for what he believed in was so great that not fighting would be a worse sin?

"This will be a good session. I can feel it," Demolache said, suddenly appearing in the room.

"Oh? And what is this one about?" I replied, taking a swig of the bottle at my bedside. I didn't even need to mix or chase it at this point. The burn felt good. I think that's supposed to be a bad sign.

"This one is about two brothers, friendship, and a betrayal most foul."

"Sounds exciting."

"Well, I like to keep you on your toes."

OZYMANDIAS AWAKENS

The sound of tree felling and sad songs filled purgatory every morning for three weeks after the Flower's fall.

Woe is me, a traveler without companion
This hole she left, my heart like a canyon.
Don't you cry, my ever lovely flower
To get you back, I'll do everything in my power.

Demolache was on a mission. Every morning he cleared
large sections of the forest. Every evening he would cut the
wood into planks, and every night he would assemble those
planks into The Grand Gesture, a giant ark he was crafting.
This was his idea to rescue The Flower. He was going to
descend back into hell to find her and then . . . He was still
working out the rest.

Through the dark beyond and more
I will fight to settle this score,
This deep pain has no cure,
Destruction only by my failure.

There was no possible way for him to return after the
descent but he didn't care. He still worked every day to build
his ark. The rest would come to him after he was reunited
with his love. He never got that chance, however. Something
else came along to distract him. While clearing the forest, he
saw a moth that led him astray. He chased it through the
woods to see where it would lead him. Eventually, he
discovered another cave, similar to his own, and decided to
investigate.

My mind is a cave, isolated and dark
My heart tender, a tree with no bark
All reminds me of your memory

I hope you, too, lament for me

"Hello?" Demolache said as he entered. "Is anyone in here?"

"Help . . . " a small voice said from within.

Demolache ventured further to find remains of a small fire and the carcasses of animals that had been consumed. It looked like a tribe had lived there a year ago. But that voice. Someone had asked for help. "Hello? Who is here?"

"Over here . . ." the voice returned.

Demolache followed a narrow path to find a dark section of the cave where a man had been cuffed at the wrists and ankles. He was feral looking and frail, but still alive. "What is this? Who are you?" Demolache had worked out that this must be where the demons had taken refuge during their stay. He wouldn't take any risks; this might be another trick.

"Please . . . need food."

"Fine. But I want answers after."

Demolache went from the cave to gather fruits from the nearby trees. The man didn't seem like a demon, but he must have known something for them to lock him up like this. He returned and fed the man by hand. He seemed to instantly bounce back to full strength.

"Now tell me, who are you?"

The man chuckled, making his shackle clank. "I am a friend, not foe. I swear."

Demolache wasn't entirely satisfied with this answer, but the demons clearly saw him as a threat and his enemies' enemy must not be half bad. "What do you know of the Demons that inhabited this cave?"

The rugged man twitched his neck to clear the hair from his face. His eyes were a deep, burning red. "They are assholes. I know that for sure."

Demolache was struck by the intensity emanating from the man. Those eyes, so familiar. "I know you. I don't know where from, but I know you."

With a cry, Ozymandias pulled at his shackles until they shattered, causing him to fall to the floor. "I would be offended otherwise," he chuckled, and then proclaimed, "I am who I am, descended from Leto, my ancestral mother, whose sons were cursed by the Divine to never create anything fruitful; not fame, nor fortune or even a daughter. I am the one destined to break this curse which forced so many of my fathers to wage others' wars upon the earth for millennia." Noticing that he failed to strike Demolache with awe, he then stated plainly, "I am the one who saved you from those waters, and I stopped you from crossing that bridge." He put his newly freed hand out for Demolache to shake.

Ignoring the rest of his statement, he grabbed the man's hand in hesitation before asking, "Why? Why did you do all that for me? What is your name?"

"My name is Ozymandias, the fated and forgotten red-eyed hero," he said as they shook. This was the first time they had ever met face to face. "Brother to Demolache, the blue-eyed god."

"Brother? God? I don't understand any of this."

"Come, let's exit this cave and I'll explain."

The two exited the cave, and Demolache showed him the way to his camp near The Grand Gesture. He had built a shack for sleeping and crates for food storage with the same lumber as the Ark.

"What is this magnificent creation?" Ozymandias asked upon seeing the ark for the first time. It was truly a spectacular feat. The shape of a strong bow with the beginnings of a house on the deck and the outline of glide wings at its side. The frame of the wings was connected to a central column that could be twisted to change course mid-flight. The entirety of the ship, including wings, was about forty feet long and thirty wide.

"The demons stole my purpose from me. I am building this to get it back."

"So that's what I've heard every morning. You are quite a devil of design aren't you?" Ozymandias chuckled.

"Stop delaying. Tell me, if you are my brother, you must know what happened! Why did I awaken on that beach? Who am I?"

Ozymandias looked him in the eye and seemed to speak to his soul. "Relaxth."

"The snake. That was you wasn't it?" Demolache realized instantly.

"Yeah. . . Just give me some time, I'll tell you everything when you are ready to hear it." Ozymandias was stalling.

Perturbed by this, Demolache sat upon the dock and looked into the abyss of clouds. The rope that held his love to his world had grown tight, and its angle seemed to drop every day. "I need to get her back."

"Why don't you just pull her up?"

"Don't you think I would have tried that already?" Demolache barked. "The rope just frays if it is pulled from this end. I fear it will break if I try to pull harder."

The two sat in silence for a while. Ozymandias broke the silence first. "Is she really worth it?"

Another few moments of silence had passed before Demolache responded. "What do you mean?"

"You don't have a way back. Is she worth risking all of this for?" Ozymandias replied.

"I honestly think she is. She was everything to me. She still is, and I treated her like an object. Locked her in a castle and guarded her. I was the dragon. Like Hades, my black heart had trapped her in Hell. Persephone, forgive me. I just want her back so I can tell her what she means to me. How much I care about her. I would love her forever if I could just hold her one more time."

Ozymandias peered into the sky. He clenched his fists at first and then relaxed. "Okay then," he sighed. "Let's build an ark."

"You're going to help me?"

"Sure, it's not like I'm doing anything else right now."

Demolache smiled. "Thanks," he said after a moment.

"For what?" Ozymandias asked, as if not realizing that he was actually doing something nice.

"Understanding . . ."

They spent the next two weeks constructing the ark slab by slab. When they were done, she was truly a sight to behold. The Grand Gesture. The ultimate symbol of loyalty. It was a scheme to read about in fairytales, but they had done it in real life. Well, metaphorically. Would it be enough? Could it really bring calm to Demolache's pain?

REPENTANCE

"I'm coming for you."

"I told you to wait for me."

"No, I can't bear to see you fall any farther."

"I swear I'm fine. Are you okay?"

"Of course I am . . . I'm fine . . ."

"You're scaring me. You know I love you, right?"

". . . and I loved you . . ."

THE TRUTH ABOUT DEMOLACHE

A week before the voyage, the duo were celebrating their success over a bonfire and a few beers. Their bond had grown strong from each telling stories of excellence from their pasts. Ozymandias told his brother of how he once got laid after winning a bar fight and how, without his friends, he would surely have lost. Demolache told him of how he saved The Flower from the bull of heaven. The details of the bull's death sent shivers down Ozymandias spine and made his left shoulder ache. Most of their stories were oddly similar in this way. But whenever Demolache would get suspicious of this fact, Ozymandias would just reassure him that, as brothers, they must have been closer than they realized. Everything was going well for the two until Demolache decided to amend his plans.

"Ozymandias, my brother, you have to come with me. Who knows what adventures lie below? We can truly fight together as we were meant to. It will be amazing," Demolache said after a few beers.

"No, no," Ozymandias chuckled. "This is your fight now," he said with a sigh.

"What do you mean? We built this ark together, and I would be a fool not to take someone of your greatness on as my crew."

"Demolache, I helped you build this ark because I gave up." He let out a half sad, half proud smile. "It's your time to shine. I'm not going to fight anymore."

Demolache looked at him, puzzled. "What are you saying? Gave up on what?"

Ozymandias sighed and threw his beer over the edge. "Have a seat," he said with a heavy heart. "There is something you need to hear."

Demolache, lighting a cigarette, sat on the floor. The cheerful mood began to die down.

"You had asked me where we came from three weeks ago. Well, I think you are finally ready to hear it . . ." Ozymandias spoke from his heart with great sadness. "We are two parts of the same whole . . . only . . . I was born, and you were created."

"What are you talking about?"

"Let me finish. Six years ago, our grandfather became very ill. I couldn't bear the pain of it all. I had always been such a narrow-minded person, always shooting forward and never looking back. When he was diagnosed, well . . . That was the first time I ever looked back. I stopped and looked at everything I had accomplished and realized it was meaningless if it could all be burned away in an instant. I wanted a purpose."

"I don't understand. Why does that have anything to do with me? Who am I?"

"Well, I thought I found a purpose. God. Somehow, I knew he had a plan for me. I was willing to accept it. But . . . Instead of saving my grandfather, he did nothing. He let him die. I was so baffled by this. I started to drown. I could no longer take the stress and pressure of the world. I . . . changed. I grew angry and cursed Him. I threw his plan against a wall and ran. I wasn't strong enough to move forward anymore. Not by myself. All the pain, all the stress, all the fear at not knowing how things would end, I hid away in a journal. I trapped you inside of a book, Demolache. I tried to, at least. You started popping up to save the day every time I had a moment of weakness, and I let you. My eyes flickering blue. I let you get this powerful. I nurtured this lie that you would find a purpose and that everyone else was wrong. Everyone else was a sinner. Then, one day, there was no me anymore."

"I don't . . . I still don't understand. Then why am I . . . How can we both exist? I am conscious, Ozymandias. I am not just an idea!"

"You became so powerful; your lies, your anger; that I could no longer control you and you became . . . another person entirely."

"I don't believe you. This is crazy. I feel, I think, I love."

"It is crazy, and I don't understand it either. I've been fighting you for so long that it just doesn't make any sense to me anymore, but it's true."

"So what? You were waiting to drop all this on me? Did you expect me to accept this and just disappear?"

"No. The opposite. You have found happiness, Demolache. I just wanted to know that it was real and not just another lie before I left for good."

"I don't believe you! You're just another demon I must dispose of!" Demolache bellowed as he clenched his fists. It was a lot to take in, one day discovering that you were just a figment of someone else's imagination.

"I don't need for you to believe me, I just need to know that you can handle reality on your own. Without my help."

"I've been through so much pain, so much torment and now this!" He began to weep in his intoxicated state.

INTERMISSION

I opened my eyes to find myself alone in my room. I didn't know what to think. I went over to my desk and started rifling through the drawers. Underneath piles of old receipts, notebooks filled with lecture notes and the occasional doodle, I found a black spiral bound notebook. After a minute of hesitation, I began flipping through pages and reading to myself aloud:

Log 3.3.10

Why?

This question provoked religion's creation. Yet this question, despite the multitude of answers, remains unsatisfied in my soul. I wish I could believe that when curtains close, it's really over. I can't do this. I find myself often staring at my hand and saying, "I control this, how could it ever end?"

I feel like why is the real question at the center of everything. When you boil everything down, it is not how did we get here or what happens to us. It is simply, "Why?"

I flipped through some more pages:

Log 4.12.10

Blind?

Someone told me today that religion was a blind walk of faith.

I responded by asking him how he knows he is on the right path if there are so many. Being blind doesn't help much either. His response was that he can "feel it."

I let my cynicism take over the conversation while I thought about this more deeply. Perhaps faith is a gift. A gentle nudge in the right direction. I was never nudged, merely thrown in a direction by my family. Who am I supposed to receive this gift from? I'm going to need to see the return address.

"This one is about Wood . . . I remember now," I said as I turned a few more pages. They were all in there. Rin, Khat, Resh, Cat, Edward had a few entries. Everything Demolache remembered in those first two years came from this journal. The next one to catch my eye was this:

Log 01.23.12

Hunger

There is a hunger within all men. Beyond tangible desires, we seek truth. We hunger for it. Truth in the form of purpose. We seek to answer the question "Why" in a more personal sense. Some are content with adopting a major religion, but religion is just a drug. It is an easy way to ebb the pain.

I say, however, that there is a beauty in starvation. There is a beauty in feeding the pain. No one should be hungry forever, but we should all know what it feels like to starve. We can't accept religion because we are pressured to feed the hunger. If God gave us free will then we should appreciate it. Such beauty in suffering is destroyed by the gluttony of those who seek the easy way out.

"What the fuck?" The image of Demolache destroying the city was instantly evoked. I flip to the very last page. It sent shivers down my spine.

Log 4.1.12

Freedom

Freedom is an arbitrary concept with no real limits. It is elusive, and yet we chase it to no end. The freedom I chase is freedom from God. I was shackled for so long by curiosity that freedom didn't seem possible. But on this night, I tasted freedom. I found it in a few brief moments of contentious thought. For those few moments, I was as happy as I used to be. For those few moments, I no longer had a chip on my shoulder. Nothing to prove, nothing to create. Just blissful contentment. For a few moments, whether God existed or not was irrelevant. All that mattered was being fulfilled. For those moments, I was. I was no longer on a bridge but on an island floating in the breeze.

"It's true . . ." I said, dropping the notebook to the floor. "Demolache's story about my life and Ozymandias' explanation of Demoloche's existence. All of it . . . is true." For a moment there, I was filled with complete horror. Had I actually forgotten about all of this? It was as if the last six years were a big blur. A blur that I was only just now beginning to see through. Who had I become? This pain had turned me into some sort of monster . . .

LOVE'S BETRAYAL

Demolache had passed out near the fire, but Ozymandias was deep in thought. He reflected upon all that he had been before his grandfather had died. He was going to conquer the world. Grand Judicar, his destiny. He was going to create something that would transcend his death and create a legacy. What was the purpose of any of it, though? It was all progress for the sake of progress. Raw ambition. Demolache had been supposed to fix that. He was going to give meaning to my actions. Motivate my ambitions with something greater than just ambition. All Ozymandias wanted was something to believe in, and it cost him the life he was meant to have. Now there was nothing left for him but to make sure Demolache was ready to take on reality alone. And after that, he was to simply fade into the abyss.

Although he had accepted this, he remained awake. He wondered. Was this really what the fates had decided? Did they choose Demolache because I had cursed my fate that day? No. This needed to be his decision. If Ozymandias was going to die once and for all, it was going to be with his consent. He stood up in the night and gazed upon The Grand Gesture. How could a man so discontent with everything fall so deeply for a flower?

Between the chirps of crickets and tweets of birds, one caught his attention. It sounded like it was saying, "Forewarn, forewarn." He ignored it, however, assuming it was in his imagination. He closed his eyes, attempting to clear his mind and get some rest . . .

Before he knew it, however, a bird had landed on his chest, calling to the heavens, "Forewarn, forewarn!"

"Out, damn omen!" Ozymandias screamed, shooing the bird from his chest.

"Forewarn, forewarn!" it called. "All is not as it seems, Forewarn!"

Startled by the omen, Ozymandias began to panic. "What is the meaning of this?" he whispered to the sky, attempting to not wake Demolache. The bird flew into a well-beaten trail through the trees.

He grabbed a lit branch from the pit and made his way into the forest, following the bird. Branches and leaves seemed to block his way as he tripped over rocks and roots. Before he knew it, he had lost sight of the bird and was just wandering the path. It wasn't long before he found himself in front of Demolache's cave. "Is this . . . What is going on?" With great hesitation, he entered. The walls were littered in letters and photographs. The letters all ended in "Love Forever" and "Your Swan." The pictures depicted the two in an embrace. It was a honeymooner's paradise. The two seemed inseparable . . . except . . . Something was off. The Flower looked happy, but Demolache seemed tired. There was a small inconsistency in his smile that only a brother would notice. Demolache was not as happy as he pretended to be, but that didn't make sense. "Why?" he demanded at the pictures. "Why build the ark? Why fight so hard if you weren't happy?" He took a letter off the wall and read it aloud.

Where art thou My Swan?

For only when we are together am I whole. As darkness seeks light, as a moth wanders, my heart seeks you. You are the divine personification, the object of my journey, the key to my forever. I have seen eternity through your eyes. I have seen fulfillment in your every act. You are my Lavinian shore. My Ithican palace. Atop Olympus is where you belong and if you are willing, I will be your cup bearer, your muse. A canvas on which to paint your revelations. In your presence, I shall never fall again.

"God." Ozymandias shuddered. Demolache wasn't in love with this flower. He lusted after the light inside her. He was using her as a bridge to reach God. She was his tower of Babel. "This is bad." He had cast his destiny aside just to find eternity the easy way. He truly was Gilgamesh, chasing a flower to ensure his immortality. "This is so bad." With a heavy heart, Ozymandias left the cave, still deep in thought. Startled, he found the bird perched on a branch, being ominous.

"What? What the fuck do you want?" Ozymandias demanded of the bird, still angry at this revelation.

The bird just sat there.

"Is there something I missed, is there more?"

The bird cocked its head and then cawed, "Forewarn, forewarn!" it began flapping violently. "Love has betrayed Demolache. Demolache shall die."

Ozymandias gaped his mouth in horror as the bird flew into the sky. "No . . ." he managed to whisper. This just gets worse and worse, he thought.

"Betrayed, Demolache shall die."

NECESSARY EVILS

The trees blew violently over the island as Ozymandias paced back and forth around the fire. Demolache was still asleep, but he didn't know for how much longer. Everything he had learned sent him into a panic. The Omen had warned of Demolache's demise, and now he needed to act. To save him from the inevitable. What if this trip below was a trap? What if the knowledge of the betrayal would cause Demolache to die? What if his own actions would kill Demolache? It was impossible for Ozymandias to know what outcome would save his brother . . .

Demolache looked so peaceful asleep, his beer still in hand. He didn't deserve anything that had happened to him. It was all Ozymandias' fault. All the pain, all that anger. It was his own pain and anger that he wasn't strong enough to handle. Now what? Now all he had left in the world was a perverse, God-lusting relationship with a woman who had abandoned and now betrayed his love. No wonder he was so angry. No wonder he lived in this world in the clouds. Even in his greatest possible imagination, all he was capable of was purgatory because he didn't believe he was good enough for heaven. Like a vampire, he was stealing heaven from this poor girl. He didn't believe he was meant to be happy. You poor creature. You sad, sad boy.

After deep consideration, he knew there was something he could do. He needed to do the right thing. With a deep sigh and a last glance at his inebriated brother, he whispered, "I am sorry Demolache. I hope somewhere inside you there exists forgiveness for what I am about to do." Ozymandias lifted a knife from Demolache's person. "I hope you are strong enough to move on from this day." He walked to the edge of the dock and grabbed the rope, the last hold The Flower had to this world and to Demolache. "I am going to need you to be strong." He sawed through the rope and watched it violently flail about in the wind as it fell into the abyss. A storm began to churn above. "Maybe you will one day understand," he said, as he made his way over to the ark. "She has betrayed you, Demolache. She has killed you." He put all of his weight into his legs. "She is a false purpose, and you knew it!" He began to push as hard as he could. "You were never happy, stop lying to yourself and move on!" he screamed, as lightning struck the ark into flames, causing it to tip over the edge. Ozymandias watched the craft spin until it caught wind and smashed into the side of the island. It fell in pieces into the clouds. Hard, cold rain began to cover the island. With one more great sigh, he covered Demolache with a blanket. The fire sizzled and smoked out. Ozymandias walked into the woods until he was out of sight.

SESSION VIII: THE REBIRTH

"Knowing all of this . . . The hard decision I made, the fact that I was trying to protect you . . . Why do you still fight?" I said the next day to the shadow in my room.

There was a hesitation before a response. "I do not fight because I condemn his actions. Not anymore at least. I vie. I struggle to live. That is what things came down to."

"But didn't Ozymandias decide that you would carry on and not him? I just still don't understand how this battle escalated into what it is today."

"He said that, and then betrayed me. Just see what happens next."

TWICE ABANDONED AND THRICE BETRAYED

Demolache awoke the next morning with a terrible headache and a worse need to release. After conducting his business in the forest, he returned to his camp sight.

"So, have you thought about my proposal?" he remarked to a brother that was no longer there. Puzzled by this fact, he began to look around. Something was not right. "No . . . NO!" he screamed, upon realizing that his long labor had gone to waste. The Grand Gesture—his proud monument to his undying loyalty—it was gone. "Ozymandias!" he screamed to the skies above. He only grew angrier as he noticed that the rope holding him to his beloved had been cut. "No . . . No . . . NO!" he silently cried as he covered his face to hide the mounting assault of tears. "Why? Why have you done this?"

Devastated, Demolache began throwing everything he could lift and kicking anything that was too heavy. He continuously screamed, "Why!" through his tears. He couldn't understand why his brother would have done this. Why had he betrayed him? Then he remembered their last conversation before he had passed out. "So you think I am just an idea? You think I don't have emotions? You think I am not capable of love? Capable of feeling?" Demolache stopped crying and began to clench his fists in rage. "I will show you my feelings, Ozymandias! I will show you my WRATH!" He lifted his axe and began sprinting through the trees.

As he made his way through the thick forest, the ground began to quake and his eyes glossed over. He swung his axe violently, taking down trees with single strikes. "Ozymandias!" he screamed. "This betrayal will not go unpunished, brother!"

Ozymandias was startled awake by the quaking ground. He had walked through the night and passed out in the clearing. The shaking ground filled him with an immense fear. He got to his feet quickly and but before he could even act, he heard the rage of a god fill the sky.

"Face me, Ozymandias, and let me quell my pain with your blood!"

Ozymandias turned to find Demolache had launched himself into the sky and was hurling towards him, the axe aimed to slice his body in half. He quickly dodged as the axe hit the ground and caused the ground to crack and tremor. Next to land was Demolache himself. His eyes were glowing hot blue rage.

"Let me explain, brother. I did only what I thought needed to be done!" Ozymandias pleaded.

"No! I am done listening to you. Brothers do not betray each other. Brothers do not lie to each other. I don't care about my origins. I do not care what you have to say for yourself. You are a monster Ozymandias, and like the rest of my demons, I must destroy you," Demolache proclaimed, lifting his axe out of the ground.

"Fighting won't solve anythi . . ." Before Ozymandias could finish speaking, he was flung to the floor by the blunt side of Demolache's axe. "Please . . . Listen . . ."

"Fight back," Demolache demanded, kicking his brother in the ribs. "Fight back, heathen."

"No . . . I won't fight you . . ." Ozymandias coughed out the words, along with a teaspoon of blood.

"Then die," Demolache murmured, lifting the axe above his head.

But before Demolache could deliver the final blow, the island quaked, throwing Demolache to the ground. He didn't get up; instead, he just lay there for a moment, trembling in pain. It wasn't a physical pain, however; it was emotional pain. He had been abandoned for the second time in his life, and it finally hit him. There was so much grief for both his grandfather and now The Flower. It was too much to bear.

Thus the two brothers lay on the ground, side by side. Neither moving, neither saying a word . . .

BROTHERS IN BATTLE

After hours of grieving, Ozymandias lifted himself from the ground and looked at his half-sane brother. "Please understand that I only did what I had to do."

Demolache turned to face Ozymandias. "Why? Why can't you let me be happy? Are you jealous? Or do you think I have not suffered enough?"

"No, none of those. Can we just leave it at that? It was for the best. Can you move on from this? Can't you find something else?" Ozymandias pleaded.

Demolache flared his nostrils and sat up. "No, not without answers. She was everything to me, Ozymandias. You know that, and yet you destroyed my chance at keeping her."

"She wasn't worth your time. We are destined for better. There will be other flowers along the way."

"I don't want other flowers."

"Do you really want to know that badly?"

"Yes."

"She betrayed us, Demolache. She abandoned and betrayed your love. More importantly . . ." Ozymandias hesitated.

The wide-eyed Demolache stood up and clenched his fists in rage. "More importantly?"

"She has killed you. I mean, not yet but . . . Because of her actions . . ." Ozymandias swallowed hard. "You will die."

Demolache's heart sank. His body went limp for a moment. He softly replied, "No . . . impossible . . ." Demolache fell to his knees. "She wouldn't. How . . ." He was clearly taking things badly. He didn't know how to feel. He didn't know how to deal with the news he had been given.

"Demolache . . . Are you going to be okay?" Ozymandias was trembling.

"Lies . . . you tell lies, heathen!" he screamed, only half believing his words. "You are just mad that your time has passed."

Ozymandias sighed deeply. "Fight me, Demolache." What else was he supposed to say? "Fight me, and if you can kill me, then this was all a lie. You can go back to your false reality and go back to believing that everything is okay. Go back to building your tower or bridge." He drew the knife that he had used to cut the rope and pointed it at his brother.

Demolache stood up, still in shock, still trembling. He lifted his axe and looked Ozymandias in the eye. "This is for everything your ambition has cost us." He attempted to scream, but his words sounded more sad than angry. He charged at his brother, swinging the axe hard at Ozymandias' arm. But in one swift motion, Ozymandias parried the strike with the knife and elbowed his brother in the face.

"Come on! This is the wanderer, the warrior, the god Demolache, where is that wrath? You aren't even trying," Ozymandias said, before licking his canine. "I sent those demons to destroy you. I caused you all this pain. Now kill me!"

"You? You let them into my purgatory? You caused all of this from the beginning? Bastard . . . Bastard!" Demolache growled and lunged at his brother. The axe lifted into the air, barely missing Ozymandias' chin, but then came down, shattering his knife and grazing his arm. The cut was deep, and blood gushed out as Ozymandias reeled back in pain.

Now unarmed, Ozymandias went on the offensive, taking advantage of the axe's momentum. He swiftly spun around and put his brother into a choke hold. The axe flew across the clearing as Demolache began to fight for air. After sustaining several painful elbows to the stomach, Ozymandias released Demolache, who responded by punching his brother in the nose. The brothers locked arms and began pushing the weight upon each other. Their eyes began to glow their respective colors. The sheer power of the two caused the ground to start shaking violently as lightning and fire started shooting from the struggle. As the two reached their zenith, an enormous explosion occurred between them, flinging them to either side of the clearing. Such power . . . I had never seen.

"You idiot . . ." Ozymandias managed to say as he struggled to rise to his feet. His nose was bloody, his arms were limp. "She played you like a fool, can't you see that? If I . . . If I hadn't sent them, you would have made a grave mistake."

"No . . ." Demolache's face was equally bloody and his arms equally limp. "Trusting you was my mistake. Your lies end now, Demon!"

The two charged at each other again, forcing themselves into a stronger stalemate. Linked by the hands and pushing with all their might, the two began to discover the true powers they had in this reality. The ground began to crumble beneath their feet as dangerous red sparks flew from Ozymandias and brutal blue embers from Demolache.

"How could you settle on something so stupid?" Ozymandias roared. "This wasn't a game! This was my life!"

"How could you betray us?" Demolache roared back. "I was finally happy! I finally had something to live for!"

"It. Was. A LIE!"

The crash this time was so immense that it flung the two brothers out of sight from each other in a white hot flash. They both lay unconscious for days on either side of the forest . . .

THE WRATH

"It's true isn't it?"

"Please listen to me! It's not how it seems!"

"You bitch!"

"We need to talk about this . . . I still care about you!"

"Don't even say that."

"I want to see you! Please be okay till I get back?"

"You are dead to me . . . Dead!"

OZYMANDIAS' RESOLUTION

"Oh my, what have we just witnessed?"

"Had the brothers not been in peace just a week ago?"

"How will this quarrel end?"

"Oh fuck . . ." Ozymandias said as he regained consciousness to the sight of three owls flapping around him and landing in a tree. "What do you guys want? Haven't you fucked me over enough for one lifetime?"

"Have we? I had not realized."

"What do we want? You aren't even sure what you want."

They giggled in unison. What assholes.

"What will we ever do with you, Ozymandias?"

The troublesome trio began to hoot in united laughter again.

Ozymandias rose to his feet. He felt like he had just been struck by a train. "Look, you guys know how this all ends, so let's just get this over with. I don't want to play these games. Just tell me what you want and why are you here."

"Well, we had come to take you away."

"Is this not the day of the grand adventure?"

"Will you not be joining us after all?"

Shit, Ozymandias thought to himself. They were right. This was the day the Grand Gesture was to set sail into the great white unknown. He had resolved to die on this day and let Demolache live. "I can't."

"Had you not decided to die on this day?"

"Is this not the day that Demolache wins once and for all?"

"Will you be changing your mind?"

"I . . . I can't let him . . . I need to do something," Ozymandias struggled to say.

"What's that? Has he said what we never thought he'd say again?"

"Ozymandias, spit it out. What do you want?"

"Will Ozymandias for the first time in five years choose . . . to live?"

"Yes . . ." Ozymandias choked out.

The Owls looked at each other and smiled.

"Is this not the Ozymandias that so long ago wanted to die? Has he changed in that five years' time?"

"Scream it loudly, Ozymandias, we are a bit hard of hearing."

"Will you not call it to the heavens?"

Ozymandias began to grind his teeth and clench his fists. It felt so good to say. "I want to live again! I want to start over! I need to undo all of his mistakes and take my life back into my own hands. I need to make things right! I want to live! I want to live!" The air grew still and the island silent. Trees stopped moving, and not a single leaf fell. It was as if time itself had stopped for a moment. "And if I do . . . I will fulfill my destiny. I promise this time. I'm sorry for running away."

In one great grin, the three moved together, and their heads began to fuse together again. "If you [had willed/will/will] wish to live again, then there [had been/is/will be] one more thing you must [have done/do/will do.] To kill the monster inside is to free the man from the misery." They let out a big chuckle as they ascended into the heavens and time began to flow again.

"I knew that already. I need kill Demolache. Once and for all."

DEMOLACHE'S RESOLUTION

Ozymandias made haste towards the other side of the island, looking for some trace as to where Demolache had landed. If he were lucky, he would find him still unconscious, and this would be easy. Or would it? The question was irrelevant, however, as he realized once he made his way to the clearing where they had recently fought. Above the trees and dancing into the sky was a cloud of deep black smoke. He knew it had to be him. "Demolache," he said under his breath. He made his way towards the smoke and slowly realized the source. It was the cave that Demolache and The Flower had inhabited for the last two years.

"Demolache!" he shouted upon his approach to the cave. "Come out and face me!"

The fire, to his surprise, was coming from inside the cave itself. As if it were the entrance to hell, the flames shot out and danced inside. Nothing the two kept sacred would emerge recognizably. Neither would Demolache.

"Demolache?" Ozymandias said as he attempted to approach the inferno.

Just as he spoke a figure appeared in the flames. "I was so wrong . . ." the figure said. "Everything is wrong."

Ozymandias gaped at the horrendous sight that Demolache had become. His skin was charred and barely still connected to his body. Muscle and bone pierced through as he walked. The island shook as the figure emerged from the cave. "What in Dido's name has happened to you?"

"Brother," the creature spoke. "I have seen the world below." The island continued to shake violently as the intensity of his voice rose. "I have seen what YOU call reality . . . and it is flawed." Demolache raised his still burning hands in the air. "But now . . . I see something else . . . light . . . I can fix it . . . I can change these monster-infested lands into a city of God!"

Ozymandias watched the figure in horror for a moment. "What the fuck are you talking about?" he said when he finally snapped out of his trance.

"Look at me brother . . . I am the wrath of God! And I will destroy all that is imperfect in this world until I have created heaven itself! That was our destiny, wasn't it? Grand Judicator?" The island began falling apart, chunk by chunk into the clouds below. "I am reborn . . . truly a god of my generation, and I will purge this world with a fire of evil and sin."

"Just calm down, Demolache! You are going to kill us both. And it's pronounced Judicar," Ozymandias screamed over the sound of the earth shifting and shattering. The sky above began to brew a violent storm.

"I will not calm down!" Demolache screamed. "I am a man twice abandoned and thrice betrayed. It's time to exact my revenge on the people who did this to me, the people that created such hatred and disdain for humanity. These monsters act for only themselves with little care about the effects. Society is flawed. Man is flawed. I will correct reality to my will because I cannot sustain my own version forever."

"You are fucking crazy! It isn't supposed to be about revenge! You're not a god, you're just a pissed off zealot with nothing better to do but fight for stupid things!" Ozymandias screamed back. "This must end Demolache. I want my life back. I want freedom from you! I want to fucking live again without you ruining everything!" He charged at the mass of flesh but was soon caught off guard by the clumps of earth that crumbled beneath his feet. The island finally gave way and like an asteroid collapsing under its own density began to crumple toward earth. The last thing Ozymandias saw was his brother enveloped in blue flames . . . Floating down to the city below.

"You bastard!" he cried out as he fell.

SESSION IX: THE RESOLUTION

I spent the next two days cowering in a ball under my sheets, rocking back and forth. My only source of nutrition was carry-out and another two bottles of whiskey. I spoke no words during that time. I just experienced fits of rage and/or tears. What the fuck was going on inside my head? I had never felt this way before. I was so scared and so angry at the same time. Their battle had actually left me paralyzed and mute. When was this story going to end? Who would I be when it finally did?

THE CITY OF DEMOLACHE

In the smoldering embers of a city in ruin, a place where all hope had been destroyed, Ozymandias awoke after the destruction of purgatory. Covered in ash and blood, he stood to see the horror that lay before him. "What the fuck?" he said, as he saw slashed-apart bodies lining the streets. Puddles of blood and gore moved in slow streams toward the storm drains as the sky slowly blanketed the city in ashes. This terror, this madness, it had only one name: Demolache.

Ozymandias made his way through the streets, looking in the windows of still burning buildings to see any sign of life. There was nothing. The wrath had completely annihilated anything that remained in this city. Woman and children, in parts. Their heads . . . They carried the horror in their eyes into the afterlife. So much blood. Limbs littered the road as if they had been cut off trying to defend themselves. He could only hope that at least some had escaped, someone, some hope. If they did, they wouldn't have gone unscarred, however; the shear amount of destruction and death was too much even for Ozymandias to handle. He eventually found himself kneeling in brain matter, tears streaming down his face. "Why? Why did I let this happen?" he whispered to himself. "How could this monster be a part of me?"

Ozymandias thought back to the beginning of Demolache's life. The days that Demolache himself didn't even remember. Buried so deep. A bottle of emotions compressed and so dark in his heart. He had been a volcano, rumbling, rumbling until eruption. This city was his Pompeii. Was it over now then? Would his heart lay dormant from this moment on? No. There is no way to control the volcano. Demolache needed to be extinguished for good. Nothing could remain if Ozymandias was to return to his former glory.

He stood up, proud to have fought Demolache instead of leaving him to pursue whatever twisted precept of good he may have found. He now wanted to finish the fight. He was going to kill a god of his own creation. Ozymandias walked through the City of Demolache with a renewed sense of purpose. He clenched his fists and licked his canine. He removed his shirt and took the knife to his shoulder, drawing the Epiphany Cross in his own blood. It would forever be his symbol of hope. Never look back, Ozymandias. Never dwell on things you can't change. You are Man, your limits are only what you accept to be boundaries. Your pain is only what you accept to feel. Your ambition is the only measure of your greatness. *"Taurus caeli illis Fiam! Let this dark mark forever be the symbol of my operas inclyta!"* he screamed to the heavens as blood crawled down his arm like a phalanx into battle. Like Manlius Torquatus before him, he marched on; fearless as a Roman commander.

Contra virum, the deity Demolache sat in the middle of a square on a throne of corpses. His dual hook-handled blades at his side, a cigarette in his right hand, and a bottle of whiskey in his left. He was waiting. There was not much else left for him to do but to wait. Self-exalted to the highest being in his mind, he had destroyed all sin, all imperfection, in his city. One thing remained, however. A man from his past. The one and only, King of Kings. A man who once saw himself as the cure for everything evil in this world. A man who Demolache knew would stand in his way of making his utopian city a reality. "You crazy bastard, you actually think this is a model for society?" he imagined Ozymandias would say. "Yes, I do," he would reply. In Demolache's mind, all he had done is cleanse the city of everything imperfect or immoral. He hadn't necessarily intended to hurt anyone. He wanted to make the city better. No, he wanted to make the city perfect. It wasn't his fault that these people were wrong. They were foolish. Full of false hope and sin. He hadn't forced them or even encouraged them to be that way, they just were, and this one-time volcano of emotions had become too cold to see things any other way. Such a waste, he had thought to himself as he cut man, woman, and child to pieces with a grand smile.

When Ozymandias finally saw the man himself sitting upon that mass of flesh, he hesitated for a moment. He had been ready for this a minute ago, but seeing the beast literally sitting upon the corpses sent shivers down his spine. What the fuck had happened? How could I have begotten this in my head? There is something seriously wrong with me, he thought.

"Why?" Ozymandias finally said upon approaching the throne.

Demolache was caught off guard at first, not seeing his enemy until he spoke. "Look who finally made it to the party," he said with a chuckle, turning to face Ozymandias. "Why? Because this city was flawed. I made it perfect."

Ozymandias' jaw dropped with shock. "You monster! There is no one left! Who is this city for if you killed all the inhabitants? Yourself?"

"Eventually, the right people will come. If I judge them fair enough, I will let them stay, but for now, it's just you, me, and the birds, dear brother." Demolache laughed harder as if life itself were a big joke to him.

"Do not call me that! Brother implies that on some level we are equal. We are nothing alike, Demolache. You are a monster, and I am ashamed to have ever created you!" Ozymandias screamed back.

Demolache laughed no more. "You created me because you weren't strong enough to move forward. You created me as your successor. If anything, I am an improved version of you. I have perfected Ozymandias. I am stronger. I am better than you. Accept that."

Ozymandias' head dropped. "I needed you once. I created you because I needed you. But I never imagined any of this would happen. I never knew how angry I was. How great my pain was. But I don't need you anymore. I don't want this to happen. The city of Demolache will never see the light of reality."

"Like I give a fuck about your opinion."

"What would you say if he could see you now? Would you show him how big your fangs were? How big of a monster you have become?"

"I would have nothing to say! Nothing to hide! I am what I am. Nothing can change that now. Nothing can change what I've become or what I must do now."

"Not even for her? Your Flower, your Swan, your Israel who you swore to love no matter what? What if she were yours again, would that change you? Huh? Would you call off your flood if she came back right now, right here? Would you lay down your blades?"

Demolache opened his mouth and peeled back his smile to show his top row of teeth. He giggled the insane laughter of a man taking pleasure in his own pain. His eyes were fixed on an unmoving point. "Nope." He giggled again. "No, I would not." He leaned in and whispered, "Honestly, I would wring her pretty little neck."

Ozymandias shuddered with horror. A deep pain shot down his spine.

Demolache screamed to his brother, "I would strangle that bitch! And when she went limp, I would bore my teeth into her breast. I would tear her still beating, warm, and traitorous heart right from her ribcage with my jaw alone. Is that what you want? The truth?"

"You monster! A beast beyond salvation! Beyond redemption!"

"As if you believe in redemption! Besides, what are you going to do about it? Kill me? You said it yourself, I don't exist. That makes me immortal!"

"I'll find a way, and if I fail, then I'll lock you so deep in my heart that you'll never see the light again. I will never let you hurt innocent people. I will never give up hope, Demolache!"

Demolache jumped from his throne, dropping his cigarette and bottle. The glass hit the pavement in slow motion. The impact of it all. The glass so fragile. It shattered into fragments as easily as did my phaneron. Shards in all directions with no central pull and no purpose. It reminded me of that moment when I had hit reality. When I realized nothing in this world could be held indefinitely. When I had shattered. Had I ever really grieved? Had I ever really moved on?

"You fucking prick! This is exactly what you want! A city where you can depend on everyone to do what's right! A city without chaos! A city where people can be free to pursue their ambitions without harming each other!" Demolache bellowed, drawing his blades.

"At what cost?" Ozymandias replied. His arm was still bleeding from the mark he had made on his shoulder. "You aren't freeing these people! You are holding them to impossible standards! Holding them accountable for being human! Have you no sympathy? Did I not teach you that you, too, are guilty of those same sins? Demolache, I am ordering you to back down." With those words, the air fell still. There was only silence; no more fires no more ash.

Demolache looked at Ozymandias with murderous intent. "What the fuck did you just say?"

"I created you. This is my life, not yours. I'm ordering you to back down," Ozymandias said with more confidence.

Demolache's face contorted with anger as he began walking towards him. "Don't you ever tell me what to do you sad sack of shit. I am a god. This is my city. You have no authority here or anywhere else."

Ozymandias drew his knife. "No, this isn't a city, you aren't a god. This is just my crazy imagination playing tricks on me. You aren't real, and you can't hurt me. Now stand down."

"I'll show you how real I am, you waste of flesh from MY past. We will see who can hurt who!" Demolache screamed as he began to charge at Ozymandias.

He whipped his swords around, and as Ozymandias parried with the knife, there was a blinding flash.

INTERMISSION

"NO!" I screamed as I awoke from the nightmare that flung my body out of bed and onto the floor. My head was pounding, and I couldn't see straight. I started crawling out of my room and towards the outside.

"Stop!" an enraged Demolache screamed as he kicked me in the ribs and onto my back. "We aren't finished yet. You can't hide from your pain any longer. No more running. Face it." He grabbed me by my collar and threw me back inside. "You can smoke once we are done."

THE BROTHERS COMPROMISE

Now locked in battle, the brothers jumped and slashed at each other furiously, neither landing a single blow. Embers and lightning flared together like fireworks in the night sky.

"You never loved her!" Ozymandias screamed as he kicked his brother to the ground.

Demolache let out a growl and jumped at his brother in response, slashing a gash through his chest.

Ozymandias cried out in pain, clutching the wound that slowly healed itself.

"You never knew her! Our love was destined, and we were perfect for each other!" Demolache belted out.

In a burst of lightning, Ozymandias charged at his brother full force, piercing his brother's shoulder. "I saw the pictures," Ozymandias said. "I know."

Demolache burst into flames, throwing his brother back, the knife still in his shoulder. He dropped his blades and removed the knife. "Maybe we were just never meant to be happy, Ozymandias. Maybe that was the closest we were to get. You ruined it with your demons!"

"NO! You gave up on your mission and took the easy way out!" Ozymandias screamed back.

They were now both unarmed and throwing fists at each other. Though much damage was inflicted, each wound just slowly healed. They fought hand to hand, endlessly, until Demolache finally got the upper hand a week later.

"Are you finished yet?" Demolache screamed as he kicked his brother in the ribs over and over again.

"I'll never . . ." Ozymandias coughed out blood with his words, "let you win."

With that, an exhausted Demolache sat down on the ground with his brother. "This war cannot be won here it seems," he said, after a moment of catching his breath.

"What do you mean?" Ozymandias replied, attempting to sit upright.

"Think about it. We have kicked the shit out of each other for several cycles, and yet neither of us can die. Face it, we aren't allowed to die yet," Demolache said, laying himself on the ground and lighting a cigarette.

"How else can we settle this?" Ozymandias replied, getting to his feet, not suspecting the treachery that was about to ensue.

"Reality," Demolache whispered. "Let us battle this out in the real world, a game of wits."

Ozymandias stared at his brother. Had Demolache not realized that he had had him on the ropes just a minute ago? He had been winning, but he had decided to stop and propose this new game. "I don't understand," he finally said.

"Think about it. We both back off and try to convince the other to our side. Like a tug of war, conducted in full conscious mind," Demolache said with a grin.

Ozymandias let out a great sigh as he helped his brother off the ground. They were both so exhausted. "Okay," he said, and with a handshake, my life became a living hell for two months. Demolache had tricked him into freeing him. The subconscious power of Demolache would now be able to interact with my reality.

LAST INTERMISSION

"So . . . that's your story," I say, returning from smoking in the winter cold. "Demolache . . . I don't know what to say . . ." I went back to my bed and lay down. Over the past two weeks, he had shared a fantastical perspective on my life with which I had begrudgingly sympathized. I understood where he came from and how he had reached his conclusion. I had watched his transformation from hero to villain, and I couldn't blame him for it. His pain was my own. His anger, too. I got it. There was only so much pain a man could take before he broke. For both of us, all it took was the final betrayal, the betrayal of myself. I snapped because I couldn't reconcile who I was with who I thought I wanted to be. For six years I had thought that I was someone else, and it had finally come back to kick me in the ass. "What now? You want to make the City of God here? On earth? Destroy a whole population to reconstruct your own paradise?"

There was no answer. The black figure on the other side of the room just approached slowly.

"There is no way I am going to let you do that! You are crazy. Did you think that understanding your pain would convince me to choose your side over his? No. This is insane, I'm not doing it."

The figure began to pace back and forth. Five a.m. again.

"I'm going to sleep. Fuck you and all of this."

As I rolled over and closed my eyes, I sensed the figure's presence standing over me. I turned over, but as soon as I did, I felt the cold, clammy palm on my neck. I started to squirm, but the more I fought, the stronger the grasp was. I began to gasp and reach. Was this my own hand on my throat? Its eyes . . . This wasn't Demolache. They were red . . . Ozymandias!

"Then you understand why I need to finish this. Stop fighting me," he said with his hand still on my throat. "If you honestly believe he is crazy, if you honestly think he is wrong, then let me win. Tonight. Don't sleep until this is over! I can do this. Even if it means . . . Even if it means facing my destiny. I can accept that now. It's what I need to do."

I nodded my head violently, but as I did, Ozymandias was ripped away and thrown across the room. Demolache was here too. I closed my eyes, and they were back in the city, fighting once again.

THE CITY OF OZYMANDIAS

They had rested long enough while battling wits in reality and now the brothers were back at it more violently than ever. They threw each other back and forth across the city, tearing flesh from each other's bodies and tossing them into the now turbulent wind. A great storm brewed above as the city shook into pieces. Could this reality be destroyed too? I filled with fear as I imagined what might lie further below. I was here, though, watching them fight. As they clashed above my head, their blue and red auras blazing about, I wondered how I had ever fallen this far. I walked the streets, looking at all that I had brought down with me. All that I had suffered in the wake of my own internal destruction. The blood. The body parts. Just let me win, Ozymandias had said. If only it were that simple. If only I could just go back to who I had been and accept this path that had been laid out for me.

"This is not the life I wanted!" Ozymandias screamed as he kicked Demolache to the ground.

"No, this is the life we were given," Demolache replied, punching his brother into a building.

I never asked for any of this. I never even asked to be born. I was induced. Two weeks late and they forced me out. Why couldn't they have just left me alone? To rot and calcify in the only place I have ever found peace? I left the womb moving forward and did so for fifteen years before I ever looked back.

That day six years ago that changed everything; why did he have to die? Why would he make that decision? Was he not strong enough to deal with the pain?

There was a great crash of a building starting to collapse as Demolache's limp body flew through the other side.

"I make my own destiny, I am in charge of my fate!" Ozymandias screamed.

Demolache lunged at his brother from the rubble. "They will take everything from you!" he shouted, tackling his brother into the pavement. "Our only fate is to die one day," he screamed, as he pounded his brother's face in.

I couldn't bear all of this anymore. I took a deep breath. "This ends tonight!" I screamed at the top of my lungs. The brothers stopped and looked at me. They hadn't noticed I was here until now. "I never wanted any of this. I just want to put all of this behind me."

I opened my eyes to find myself in my room.

"I have become a monster. I want to go back to who I was. I don't want this anger anymore. I don't want to be the villain of my own story."

I had hoped that would stop things, but all I felt was a shudder as I imagined the two bursting through my wall, still in combat. It wasn't enough to just choose. I had to end this myself. I had to become my own answer.

"You are not alone," said a voice sheathed in mist as he entered the city. It was Wood, and he wasn't alone either.

"We are here for you, great adventurer," Rin said.

Resh said nothing. Instead, he lifted the left sleeve of his robe to reveal the Epiphany Cross on his shoulder. They all did.

Cat, Edward, the savages. Tor and Ret, John. They were all here in the city, brandishing the Epiphany Cross.

"Fight your demons, Ozymandias. We believe in you," Khat said, emerging from behind the group and palming the cross with his right hand.

"So you've brought an army have you?" Demolache snickered.

"No," I said. I had made my decision. "No more pain, Demolache. No more regret. This is who I am. This is who I will always be."

"NO!" Demolache screamed with a great rage. "No, I am who you are now, I am the result of everything that has happened to you!"

"They aren't here to fight you, they are here to watch me. They are here to help me remember," I said with a new sense of pride.

"You can never go back to that day. You can't change everything that has happened!" he screamed in protest.

"I know, but I can move forward. I can forgive, forget, and love again. I will never again let my demons control me. That ends with you. Here. Tonight." As the words left my mouth, a ray of sun shone through the clouds and began to dissolve the city.

"Fight me one last time then. Fight me as a demon if that's what you believe I am. And when you realize that you can't kill me, then you will understand that I am not the same as those others," Demolache demanded.

I opened my eyes to find Demolache mid-punch in my room. His fist crashed into my ribs. This wasn't real; how could he hurt me?

"Get the fuck up and fight me!" Demolache screamed as he threw me out of bed.

"How are you doing this?" I cried as I coughed and lifted myself to my feet.

"Because this pain, this anger, everything you feel, it is real! That is what I am trying to show you. I am real, Ozymandias, I am real!" Demolache screamed. He grabbed my left hand and shoved it into his heart, and it began to burn.

"Fuck!" I screamed in pain as I pulled my hand away. "This can't be happening, you can't really be here!" I thought when I made my decision, he would just disappear. How wrong I was. How right he was. My pain, it was real.

He punched me in the nose, and I stumbled back. "Fight me, you coward! Fight back!" he screamed as he hit me again and again.

"No! I will not fight you anymore. I will not fight."

This was all in my head, he couldn't really hurt me. With every punch I sustained, however, I believed myself less and less. What was it that had made me so strong before? What had allowed me to face my pain?

"You're losing a lot of blood, are you sure you don't want to fight back?"

It was them. The people. I knew they had my back. They always would. I thought about all the people I had in my life. Friends, family, lovers. I had felt so alone for so long, but I had never really been alone. There would always be people on whom I could rely. They had helped me get this far; they could help me defeat my demons. I didn't have to do it alone.

With that thought, the pain subsided. The damage had been done. Demolache's punches and kicks were useless. They phased right through me. I remembered everything. Who I was and where I was going. More importantly, who I was taking with me. Those who had influenced me and those I influenced. I felt an eerie sense of calm, and I knew exactly what I had to do.

I grabbed my pocket knife and my lighter and began crawling towards the bathroom.

"I am going to beat this. I will destroy you," I say, still clutching my chest as I made it into the bathroom.

"What are you going to do with that?" Demolache screamed in fear.

I lifted the knife in my hand. The cold metal feel. The heft of it. Was this real or was this in my head? I honestly didn't know. I did know one thing, Demolache had to die. Here. Tonight. Before any of it came to fruition. Before I let myself fall any further. Before he hurt someone. Because inside the man lay a monster that was growing. Something evil inside him that sought destruction as its final cause. One of greater power than I could have ever imagined. He had driven me this far. He could only do more damage. "I'm going to do what he couldn't. I am going to end this," I say, as I turn the knob on the faucet, allowing scalding hot water to fill the tub slowly.

"What the fuck do you think that will accomplish? This is stupid," he said as I began to heat the metal blade to a dim glow with my lighter.

I honestly didn't know what I was doing. My hand was shaking in fear. "I'm making sure that I never lose myself to you demons again," I said, right before jamming the hot blade into my left shoulder. I cringed and cried out in pain as I drug it through layers of skin, but I didn't stop. The blade had made a clean and hot cut before I returned it to the fire. "I'm reminding myself to never look back again." The scorch of the blade was much worse than the cut as I drug it through again. I was in a trance-like state now, however, so even though the pain was unbearable, I could only smile as the Epiphany Cross began to take red and bloodied shape.

"Do you honestly think you are killing me?" Demolache yelled as he paced back and forth. Was I actually carving into my shoulder? Was this all just a hallucination? "Why would this even kill me?" he continued. "This is insane. You call me crazy, but look who's holding the knife, carving a puzzle piece into his goddamn shoulder!"

"I can't kill you. You are a part of my phaneron. I don't believe you are entirely useless either. I may need you someday," I said, throwing the knife to the ground and attempting to lift myself off the ground. "And no, this isn't supposed to kill you," I said, looking at the mess of burnt flesh and gore to my left. "That's what the water is for. Hope, Demolache. I don't know if I will survive this, but I hope I will, and when I do, you will be gone. At least I hope you will be." As I spoke, I let my body fall into the almost overfilled tub.

I screamed as I hit the water, but it was muffled by the splash. My flesh was burned in the water, yet all I could do was cringe. I held my breath for as long as I could, but the pain eventually became unbearable, and I screamed under the water. The last thing I saw before the water entered my lungs was the blood from my shoulder spreading in streaks.

SAVE ME

In my half-conscious state, I felt myself swimming through time itself. I swam through the events of the past six years until I reached the beginning of it all. At the bottom of this deep ocean was a hospital room funeral. At least, it felt like a funeral to me, as it was the last time I would see that man. I swam inside to find my grandfather lying on a gurney with my fifteen-year-old self at his side. Tears streamed down my face as the beeps slowed to a stop. "Goodbye, Nonno," I said to the withering man when the beeps stopped. The scene then rewound and the beeps started again. The boy cried and then said goodbye. I watched it over and over again, feeling overwhelmed. I didn't want to believe it had actually happened. I had trapped myself in my mind to avoid the reality. No, I'm stronger than this now. I've come so far. I swam up and grabbed the boy by the hand. There was a scream from the surface. As I pulled him out of the room, I was overcome with great anger. Why? Why had he left us all? Why did this have to happen? I was angry at myself. I had blamed myself for this. Not anymore. This was not my fault in any way. I couldn't stay mad. What else could I have done? I could have spent more time with him. Maybe I could have reassured him, encouraged him, perhaps I could have made him stronger. If only he had been stronger. Lost in my mind, I didn't even realize that the boy had started squirming to escape my grasp. He cried and hollered to go back. The boy just wanted his grandfather back. Tears began to mix with the water in my face, and I stopped swimming. I lay there crying, unable to overcome my sadness.

"Breathe," a muffled voice eventually screamed from the surface. "Please breath!" It grew louder.

I wiped my tears and grabbed the boy firmly. It was too late to question everything. It was too late to still be sad. He was gone now. I had to move on. "I must go on!" I screamed in my head and began swimming harder and faster than before, the boy still in my clutches. When I broke the surface, I gasped loudly for air, murmuring nonsense. "The demon is dead."

"Thank God," a voice said above me. All I could see was her red hair. "Hey, look at me," she said, but my eyes were unable to focus. "Look at me, you're still here, you're still you . . ."

Then everything went black . . .

EPILOGUE

Still here, she had said. Who was she? Just a bystander who had seen the open door? Or perhaps some angel come to rescue me. Still . . . me. But . . . Something was different. Same body, different . . . Soul? In my unconscious state, brought on by exhaustion most likely, I found myself in a church. It was dark, but I could see pews, the stained glass, and even an altar with a cross above it. There was something else with me in the room. A shadow in the back of the church. I approached it cautiously.

"Don't do this," the figure said. It was sitting on the ground with shackles bracing its arms and legs. After a few seconds, it lifted its head and looked me in the eyes. Blue. Demolache. "Don't become their bull."

"That's all you have to say after all you did or at least tried to do?" I scolded the shadow.

His head dropped, and he began shaking it back and forth. "You don't understand. I didn't want to hurt anyone, I never did. It was a metaphor, I was angry, and it felt good." He looked back at me, his tone changed to something more urgent. "Listen, there has to be a better way, Ozymandias.

You saw something. I know you did. I felt it when I awoke on that beach. You needed to run. There was something awful in their plans. Whatever it was, the pain of it all. It's going to be too much. I'm begging you, do not do this."

"What? I am just supposed to trust you? Believe everything you have to say now? I am honestly supposed to believe that being chained up has turned you into a noble soul who has my best interests in mind?" I continued to scold.

"Our best interests. Think, Ozymandias. What happened that day? Why did you run away? Why did you create me? Whatever it is, there is another way!" he was beginning to sound desperate.

I laughed sarcastically. "Like I'm supposed to remember that." He was right, I didn't want to remember. "And what other way? A city in the clouds? Another flower? No, Demolache, I won't waste my life with a lie."

Demolache sighed, "That's fine. You win, the future is yours." His eyes began to widen as if he were putting things together, "You're canines! Red eyes! Remember god damn it!"

"No!" I screamed back. "I won't listen to your madness any longer. I was wrong in creating you! Your tragedy is ever having existed in the first place!" I took a deep breath. "You were right about one thing, however. There is something profoundly wrong with the world. I think I can fix it." I felt my eyes begin to glow hot with ambition, "And if I have to surrender to them, then I will."

"Does this mean you are ready?" a voice spoke from behind me. I turned to see it was the middle-aged owl and the other fates.

"We had told you what you needed to do," the oldest owl pointed towards Demolache.

"You will still kill the Demolache?" the youngest added.

I looked at the knife that had appeared in my hand. It was the same knife from the city. The same that had carved into my shoulder. Or did it? Did that actually happen? I didn't know. "No. I may need him. I did at one point. I may need him again."

I looked him in the eyes. He seemed happy that I had spared him. I saw his worry, though. Maybe he was on to something.

"As long as you will accept your destiny, we will let you do what you will with him."

"We had best be going now, Ozymandias."

I shivered. "Yeah, about that . . . um . . . How will . . . I mean . . . When will I know that I'm done? That I've done your will or my destiny? Whatever it is that I am supposed to do?"

"When you beget a daughter, that is the sign that you are done. That is when you are free from Leto's curse, and your veins are purged of your taint."

I chuckled. "Seems simple enough." I had taken two steps towards them before Demolache spoke again.

"Wait!" he screamed back to me. "I won't help you. You will need me someday, and I will not help you."

I scratched my head and tried to reassure myself. "I will convince you. Somehow. I'll win you over." Two more steps.

"Stop!" he screamed again. "They know everything, ask them. Ask them how it all ends and how this actually began. I know it's terrible. Believe me, brother!"

"Shut it, shattered one! You had your chance to appease us!" the older owl snapped at Demolache.

"I will not! Ozymandias, I'll make you a deal. Ask them to show you it all. Feel the pain I felt. The whole thing. If you still decide to go through with it after seeing it all play out, I will help you unconditionally."

I turned to face him. "Is that a promise?"

"Yes," he said.

I looked into his eyes and saw his sincerity. There was no harm in asking. "O fates, servants of the divine." I turned to face the three owl-men. "Show me my destiny. Tell me what I am to do and how it all ends. Let me feel both the joys and tears of my life's work under His guidance," I said with a smile.

"That is not how this works. There are rules to our game. Rules which we live by."

"Will you actually take the advice of this false prophet monster?"

"Had you lost your mind along the way?"

They seemed oddly defensive. "You have a job to do. I could go either way. Show me or I walk," Ozymandias threatened.

The fates turned to each other and discussed.

"He is bullshitting."

"We will not take that chance again."

"Had this not been the boy who abandoned his destiny before?"

"He is too afraid to do it again. Are we really going to fall for what is obviously a ruse?"

"We had a way to do this before. A method that had still worked in our favor."

"Yes! We will obscure the future, we will blind him with uncertainty."

"He is too smart for that. He will put things together. We will fail."

"If so, then we will go with plan B. The binding contract."

The fates nodded and turned to me and then the young one spoke. "We will do what you ask if you make us a promise."

"Okay?" I replied.

"You will promise us that no matter what you see, you will not attempt to cheat us. If you do, we will abandon you forever to do battle with the cruelest chance."

I laughed at first. "You are going to give me bad luck?" They stared back menacingly, waiting for an answer. "Fine. I will obey your rules."

The fates began laughing something sinister and then grinned at each other. "All [hailed/hail/will hail] Marcus, father of Catherine, and Grand Judicar of the New World."

"What is this? Macbeth?" I laughed again at their silly chant.

The fates then flew at me all at once, causing a great gale that almost knocked me over. I fell to my knees and began to feel a great agony in my left shoulder. "I said pain and joy, did I not?" But there was only pain. It outweighed all else. I screamed and grabbed my shoulder as I fell to the ground. That damn dark mark. It burned like a thousand suns becoming a permanent fixture on my very soul. I closed my eyes and began to crawl forward against the wind.

I thought back to that hospital. Sitting in a chair. Staring at my grandfather breathing through a tube. He stared at the ceiling. Blinking and not saying a word.

My nails began to break as I continued to crawl. I felt them bleeding, and I started to cry. My tears were just swept away by the wind.

✤

"It's time to go, say goodbye." My mom entered the room and kissed her father on the head. I stood and did the same. "Goodbye Nonno," I said and walked out of the room only to sit in another chair in the hallway. My uncle was arguing with my aunts not too far away. I hung my head in misery. I reached into my pocket and grabbed the puzzle piece within it.

✤

The wind at this point began to win. I was not crawling, just holding on for dear life.

✤

"What is wrong little boy?" a nurse said to me as I was examining the puzzle piece. There are two of them. The younger one is kinda hot.

"My grandpa's sick. I keep praying, but he isn't getting any better," I replied.

The younger nurse starts rubbing my head. "I'm sure he will get better. God will have a plan for him just as God will have a plan for you."

I fake a smile.

"We had best be going ladies," an old doctor said as he walked by the nurses.

They nodded and turn back to me. "Cheer up, you are going to get through this. I'm sure you are going to be very important someday," the older nurse said as she put her hand on my shoulder.

The younger nurse said, "We'll see you around." Then they walked down the hall and into my grandfather's room.

✝

It was too powerful. I was sliding back. The floor couldn't hold me, so I grabbed onto a pew. I was in so much pain.

✝

I remembered thinking it was odd that the nurses didn't have name tags. Neither did the doctor, actually . . . I stood up and started walking to the room. Everything was silent except for the beeps of his heart monitor. They echoed through my mind as I heard them slow to a stop. When I got to the room, there was no one in there. His eyes were closed, and there were no more beeps. It hit me all at once, and I screamed in silence. I threw the puzzle piece against the wall and ran to his side, crying. I pushed him. I hit him. I demanded that he wake up. My parents grabbed me and removed me from the room. A nurse closed the door behind us. Sad, red eyes began to glow hot blue. A rage combusted inside of me. I struggled free and began running. I ran, and I ran until I saw the doctor and the two nurses outside the hospital doors.

"Where are you going?"

"We had only just begun."

"We will be watching you, Marc."

"No. No. NO!" I screamed as I continued to run. I ran so far. I ran so long. That's where it all began.

✝

I couldn't hold on any longer. My hands started slipping. I opened my eyes to the wind. I was wrong. I thought he chose to die. I thought him weak. It was them. How could I have been so blind? As I tumbled backward, I saw the Jesus upon the cross had lifted its head. I felt the eyes of the divine pierce me as it spoke, "Regnum mea veniat." With that, I was flung into the abyss . . .

I awoke screaming and grabbing at my shoulder. It hurt tremendously. I tore off the bloody bandage and saw the dark mark burned into my skin. This was no dream. In subduing one monster, I had become another. "What have I done . . ?"

Red eyes glared in the night. There was no longer anything holding me back. I burned with ambition, and to this destiny, I was fated. To the moon itself, I spoke, "Nunc, scintillae spei causa pugno . . ."